LIFE IS FOR THE LIVING

S.C. STOKES

A WELCOME & WARNING

Welcome to Life is for the Living, the most recent title in my new Urban Fantasy adventure, Conjuring a Coroner.

Urban Fantasy has always held a special place in my heart. The blend of magic and the modern world, along with a generous rewriting of history to add a hint of the arcane is incredibly addictive for me as a reader. I hope you are similarly entertained!

Are ready to get lost in an exciting new world?

The Conjuring A Coroner Series is set in New York in the year 2017. The key difference between this world and the one we live in, is the presence of magic. Where and how these worlds intersect...well, you'll have to turn the page to find out.

Enter the world of magic with Kasey Chase—she'll suck you into a realm of magic, murder, and mayhem that you won't want to leave.

I must warn you though. Kasey is far from perfect. She's an unschooled witch with unpredictable magic, a sharp tongue and a troubled past. She possesses a fierce sense of justice, and an insatiable curiosity that often gets her into trouble.

If Kasey were here, she would tell you that asking for forgiveness is far easier than asking for permission, so...buckle up; it's going to be a wild ride!

As you join Kasey on her adventure, I hope you too can look

beyond her shortcomings and see her as I see her, a diamond in the rough.

Let's do this!

S.C. Stokes

P.S. Want to be a VIP?

VIP's get early access to all the good stuff, including exclusive give-aways, signed editions, exclusive pre-release parties, and some free books! Click the link below to join for FREE.

Become A VIP - https://readerlinks.com/l/959935

CHAPTER ONE

*K*asey stood, paralyzed with fear, her heart racing. She was trapped.

All around her, the flames licked higher and higher. Heat from the swirling inferno seared her skin as it threatened to consume both her and the apartment.

She turned for the door, but the wall of flames blocked her path. Beads of sweat ran down her face. Her breathing was short and shallow as she struggled against the thick smoke.

Then, out of the darkness the shadowy figure of a werewolf charged at her through the inferno. He bowled her to the ground.

The Golden Wolf loomed over her, his red eyes gleaming as he reveled in his victory. Saliva dripped from his open mouth as he raised his paw, ready to deliver the killing blow.

Time slowed as the taloned paw descended.

Shaking her head, she shouted, "No, no, no! This isn't what happened."

Someone pounded at the door.

"Kasey, are you in there? What's going on?" a voice called, startling the beast.

"I killed you, you're dead!" Kasey pleaded as she struggled against the beast.

It was only a matter of time until flames consumed them both.

This is all wrong. Kasey grimaced as the paw sliced into her chest.

A noise startled her awake.

Her apartment faded as her eyes blinked open. She reached for her stomach and found it unscathed.

It was just a dream.

Rubbing her eyes, she sought to clear her mind of the terrifying nightmare.

Sunlight shone through the open curtains. It took her a moment to remember where she was. It had been years since she had last been in this room. The stress of her week faded as she remembered she was safely ensconced in her family's home.

The knocking continued, bringing with it the realization that it wasn't a part of her dream.

"Kasey, can you hear me?" her father yelled through the door.

Kasey called out, "Yeah, Dad, sorry. I'm here."

She scrambled out of bed, but almost fell over. Shooting pains reminded her of the very real wound Danilo had inflicted. The terrifying struggle now permeated her dreams. She had been fighting for her life when the Werewolf's claw had sliced deep into her thigh.

I must get that looked at.

Taking care to place her weight on her good leg, she hobbled over to the door.

Opening it, she found her father standing in the doorway, his brow furrowed.

"Sorry, Dad, I just had a bad night's sleep. Did I wake you?"

"Not at all," he replied, the bags under his eyes giving away the lie. He would do anything for his children.

"Just glad to see you are okay. Come on down and join us. Your mom has made waffles."

The sweet scent of toasted waffles wafted through the house. "Sure, Dad, I'll be right down. Just give me a few minutes to freshen up."

"No worries, Kase. See you downstairs." Her father disappeared down the hall.

Kasey made her way to the bathroom, smiling. Whether she was sixteen or twenty-six, nothing changed. She was still Kase to her dad.

Reaching the bathroom sink, she studied her reflection in the mirror, surveying the damage from Danilo.

It was the first time she had braved a mirror in days and she instantly regretted it. Her hair was a disheveled mess. A myriad of cuts and bruises told the tale of her fight with the killer. She had barely made it out alive.

Days of overwork and sleep deprivation had taken its toll. Heavy bags rested under her eyes. It would take a week of sleep just to catch up.

Of course, that week of sleep was a pipe dream. She couldn't stop now. Danilo might have been gone, but he was just a foot soldier. The organization responsible for the string of murders he had committed was still out there, somewhere.

Now she knew what they were after: her.

She had no idea who the organization might be, but clearly, they were involved in the pending attack on New York City. Danilo had admitted that much.

Her recurring vision of the attack had proved a threat to their plan. A threat that they would see removed no matter the cost. How much Danilo had managed to report remained a mystery, but Kasey had to assume the worst.

I'm still in danger, and I don't know who is behind it.

One thing was clear even when confronted with certain death, Danilo had been unwilling to give up anything of substance on his employers. He had feared them far more than he did Kasey.

What could inspire that kind of fear? Kasey wondered, not for the first time. Danilo Lelac had been an assassin and a Werewolf. Not only that, but he was one of the most infamous assassins the World of Magic had known. His fear of his employer only served to heighten Kasey's concerns.

She was determined to unravel the mystery. Not only had her vision of the attack on New York plagued her since she was a child but now, they had threatened her family.

I may not know who you are, or where you are, but I will end you all.

Kasey studied her battered reflection in the mirror.

With a heavy sigh, she turned on the tap and splashed water on her face to wake herself up. When that failed, she decided to take a shower. The warm water was a soothing balm on her aching muscles. Then, she followed the aroma of freshly toasted waffles down to the dining room.

The scent of breakfast assailed Kasey's nostrils. Her parents were both already seated at the table but were patiently waiting.

In the center of the table sat a tall stack of waffles. Around them lay every topping one could wish for: fresh fruit, chocolate sauce, maple syrup, and even ice cream. Her mom had clearly gone into overdrive.

A pang of guilt stabbed Kasey in the chest. In an attempt to leave the world of magic behind, she had neglected her parents as well.

She pulled out a chair and sat down. "Mom, breakfast looks amazing, thanks."

Her mother looked about bashfully. "Oh dear, it was nothing."

Kasey gestured at the mountain of waffles. "May I?"

"Of course, dear," her mother replied. "They are for you, after all."

Kasey lifted a waffle off the stack and then began scooping ice cream onto her plate. As she doused the waffle and ice cream in chocolate sauce, she looked down at the table.

"Mom, Dad, I just want to say I'm sorry," she squeezed out before her emotions welled up, choking her.

It had been an unbelievable nightmare of a week, yet amid it all her parents never ceased to amaze her. No matter how far she ran from her parents, or how neglectful she had been in her communication, their unconditional love waited, ready to welcome her home.

She sank her teeth into a large slice of waffle. The chocolate sauce rolled smoothly over her taste buds. "Mmm," she moaned.

The truth was, she'd never felt as safe as she did in her own her home. While they may not have been in the wealthy elite, the Stonemoores' reputation preceded them. Their place in history had been earned during England's Great Purge. It would be a particularly foolish or ignorant individual that chose to arouse the ire of Jane Stonemoore.

"You don't have to apologize, dear," her mother replied. "We know you've been busy. When we moved here, we knew what you wanted. Magic isn't the only path you can take. We are tremendously proud of all you have accomplished."

Glancing at the mountain of food, her mother continued, "How are the waffles? They used to be your favorite."

Kasey smiled. "They still are, Mom. Some things never change." Finishing her mouthful, she continued. "Since transferring to the NYPD, things have been a little hectic, but I'll do better at staying in touch. I promise." She looked down nervously. "I meant what I said last night. I've spent so long running away from the World of Magic that I ran away from you too. I'm sorry."

Her father smiled. "There's no need to apologize dear. We'd rather hear what you are planning to do now? Your apartment looked like a bomb hit it. You know you can stay with us as long as you need, right?"

"Thanks, Dad," Kasey said. "I have a lot I still need to sort out, but after breakfast, I have to get to the station."

"The subway, dear?" her mother asked reaching for the fruit platter.

"No, the police station," Kasey replied. "I still have some work to do."

"Come now, Kasey. You almost died last night. You can take a day off," her father said.

"I could, but Danilo's body is in evidence. I need to make sure no one finds out what he truly was. Then there is the matter of my vision of the attack. It is clear to me now. I am a witch and my gift has been given to me for a reason. That reason is to save lives.

"The vision that I have been seeing since the Academy is real. Someone is out there planning something horrible. Unless I do something about it, thousands of people are going to die, maybe more. It could be today, tomorrow, or weeks from now, but it is coming, and it's coming to New York. We're all in danger unless I can find a way to stop it."

"Kasey," her mother chimed in, "you're better off leaving those matters with the Arcane Council. They will stop the attack. They always do."

"I can't do that," Kasey replied. "For whatever reason, this gift has been given to me and I can't sit idly by. I must do something!"

Jane nodded. "How are your gifts? We haven't spoken about them in years. Your father and I figured they must've stopped when you left the Academy. It seems that wasn't quite the case?"

"They certainly slowed," Kasey answered sipping on her orange juice. "They weren't nearly as frequent as I was experiencing before, but they still happen."

"Just like before?" Jane asked.

"It started that way," Kasey said. "But now they are different. I feel like my gift is getting stronger each day. I feel like I'm understanding the context of them better than ever before. It's helping me solve cases and frankly, that makes me feel good. It makes me feel like I matter."

"Of course you matter, dear. Your father and I love you."

"You know what I mean, Mom." Kasey replied fidgeting with her fork. "At the Academy, I felt like I was just nosing about in others' business, sharing embarrassing moments that I witnessed, and being hated for it. But I'm not a child anymore, I work with the police here in one of the world's busiest cities. My gift is making a difference. It's saving lives."

"We are proud of you," her father said, "but you need to be careful. If these people were willing to send a killer after you once, they will do it again. You need to have both eyes wide open."

Kasey nodded as she finished her waffle.

"Last time, I didn't know they were coming. Now I do. This time I'll be ready." She stood up. "I don't want to eat and run, Mom, but if I don't get to the station soon, I'm worried Vida will find something on Danilo's body. I can't have him digging around asking questions. The ADI is already all over me. If our community is discovered... Well, truth be told, I don't know what will happen, but Arthur Ainsley made it clear that it would end poorly."

She turned away from the table. Her injured leg threatened to give out again.

"Oh, Kasey," her mother said, "if you are going to go tearing off again, at least let me take a look at your leg. You can barely walk, let alone rush around town."

Kasey relented. Unfortunately, healing magic was not her strong point. Having never made it to her senior years at the Academy, she had not taken the necessary classes.

If there was one time a witch's magic needed to be spot on, it was when it was interfering with the human body and its natural course. Failing to correctly enunciate a spell or even having a momentary lapse in concentration could have disastrous consequences. She had chosen to avoid any such possibility by avoiding it altogether.

Her mother sprang up from the table. In a second, she was at Kasey's side. Her mother carefully examined the wound in Kasey's thigh, as well as the myriad of cuts and bruises.

" Kasey my dear, you need to take better care of yourself. Sit down, let me handle these for you."

Kasey flopped back into her seat. "Please be careful with the healing, though. If you overdo it, you'll arouse suspicions. Maybe leave a few of them just for effect."

Her mother smiled. "Of course, dear."

She held up her hand, palm outward facing toward Kasey's injured thigh. Closing her eyes, she exhaled slowly before uttering her spell. "*Gwella.*"

Her hand glowed a golden light that radiated outward.

Kasey watched in wonder as the flesh of her thigh knitted itself together. As it did so, the dull pain which had plagued her since the night before faded until it vanished entirely.

With the thigh healed, her mother turned her attention elsewhere. Sweeping her hand over Kasey, Jane carefully guided the healing aura. As the golden light washed over her, Kasey watched spellbound as the lacerations healed, one by one.

Her mother clenched her fist and the healing glow ceased.

Kasey stretched and ventured a step. Her leg took the weight well, her thigh no longer burned with each step. Not only that but Kasey felt rejuvenated. Where only minutes before she'd been on the edge of exhaustion, now she felt like she could tackle anything.

"I feel amazing!" Kasey exclaimed as she threw her arms around her mother.

"Glad to hear it, dear, but be careful, magic is not a substitute for taking care of yourself. Eventually you'll burn out, or even worse, your body will begin to reject the influence of the healing magic and it will cause further harm."

Kasey practically bounced on her toes. "Got it, Mom, thanks!"

Her mother shook her head. "I laid out some of your old clothes, dear. They should tide you over until you're able to get some new ones. The ones you're in now..." She paused for a moment. "They aren't really fit for public use."

Kasey looked down. Her denim jeans had a large tear where Danilo's claw had sheared through them. Her T-shirt likewise was in tatters.

"Thanks, mom. Where can I find them?"

"In the lounge room. Would you like me to drive you to the station?"

Kasey was just about to turn down the offer, but she already felt terrible for her dine and dash. "Sure, Mom. That would be great. Just give me a moment to get changed."

She raced into the lounge room. Her clothes had been laid out neatly on the sofa. Immediately, she realized why she had left them at home. There were a half a dozen different sets of jeans, most of which have gone out of style in the last decade. The T-shirts weren't much better.

She sifted through the pile and found the best fit: a set of dark blue jeans and a T-shirt that she had loved as a teenager. Across its chest it had the slogan, "I'd love to have a battle of wits with you, but you appear to be unarmed."

Even now the cheeky T-shirt made her smile. She changed and headed back into the dining room.

"Thanks for breakfast." Kasey began giving her dad a quick hug.

"You're welcome, dear," Ralph replied. "Take care of yourself, okay?"

"Of course. I took down a Werewolf. After that, a phantom organization will be easy, right?" She grinned.

"Alright Kasey, let's go," her mother called. "I'll drop you off at the station and then I'm going to go visit your sister."

Kasey followed her mother out to the car. Together they chatted all the way to the station. Life had been hectic, Kasey filled her mom in on what it was like to work with the NYPD. Her mother brought her up-to-date on some of the current affairs in the World of Magic.

Pulling into the station, her mother turned to Kasey. "You need to be cautious in dealing with the Ainsley's. Arthur is a political animal. He has fought his way to the head of the Council, leaving only wreckage behind him. He has money, power, and magic. He is best avoided."

"It was never my intention to end up at odds with him, Mom. His son is a pig. I didn't even know who they were until Arthur showed up at the station. As soon as I get him to drop this lawsuit, I'll be done with the lot of them. I have far more important things to worry about than the posh end of town."

"Kasey, ever since you told us about Danilo, I've been thinking. Whoever was hunting you has tremendous reach. They were able to dig up your records from the Academy of Magic and track you here. Be careful, trust no one, not even the Council."

"You think the council might have something to do with it?" Kasey asked.

"I don't, know," her mother replied. "Just keep both eyes open, you see anything suspicious, call me. You aren't alone in this."

"I will, Mom." Kasey leaned over and threw her arms around her mother. It was awkward over the center console of the car, but Kasey persisted and drew her mother in anyway. "Say hi to Sarah and the kids for me. Langdon too, if he is home."

"He should be in later today. Sarah mentioned he was getting back from his conference in Germany. We're going to pick him up from the airport."

"Well, give my best."

"Will do, hun." Jane fixed her with a knowing stare. "If you need help, just call. We are here. You will never be alone."

Kasey popped the door open and smiled. "Thanks, Mom."

Sliding out of the car she shut the car door and made her way toward the precinct building. It had only been a day, but it felt like a lifetime ago. Pulling open the large double doors, she entered the station.

"Kasey?" a voice called across the lobby. "What on earth are you doing here?"

Kasey froze, and so did her heart.

CHAPTER TWO

$\mathcal{K}$asey searched for the source of the voice. Her hand trembled as the heavy station door pushed back against her.

Scanning the lobby, Kasey spotted Detective Bishop striding purposefully across the lobby to greet her. Bishop's forehead was creased with worry.

"I said, what are you doing here?" Bishop repeated.

Kasey cocked her head. "I work here, or at least I did the last time I checked."

Bishop smiled. "That's not what I mean, and you know it. You were almost killed last night. No one would blame you if you took a day off. In fact, the chief told us you would be taking the week."

"Well, he hasn't told me yet, so I'm here," Kasey replied, throwing her hands up and doing her best impression of a cheerleader's spirit fingers.

Bishop looked Kasey up and down. "I'm glad to say you're looking a lot better than you did last night, that's for sure."

"It's amazing what a full night's sleep and washing the blood off will do for you," Kasey replied. "So, where are we on the case?"

Bishop put her arm around Kasey and steered her toward the elevator. "Officially, it's closed. You may have missed it, but the chief did a piece on Good Morning New York this morning. With the perp on ice in the morgue, the chief wanted to get the word out as quickly as possible. The other women have been released from protective custody, as well, now that the danger has passed. Unofficially, we are just taking care of the last of the paperwork.

"Vida took some time off this morning for a personal matter, so we're still waiting on him for the autopsy. Not that we are expecting any surprises there. We got a good look last night, Kasey. Pretty sure the cause of death was the piece of steel you put through his chest before barbecuing him, that sound about right to you?"

Kasey nodded. "Pretty much, Bishop. It took everything I had but it was him or me."

Bishop's face was difficult to read but the glistening in the corner of her eye told Kasey all she needed to know. Bishop was still upset about Collins.

Before the killer had revealed himself as Danilo Lelac, they had known him as Agent Collins and believed him to be a liaison assigned to the case by the FBI.

Collins and Bishop had got on like a house on fire. Unfortunately for Bishop, Collins had turned out to be a sociopath and a serial killer. As muscle for hire, he had been paid to hunt down Kasey. He had almost succeeded, but Kasey had emerged from the burning apartment victorious and Danilo Lelac was no more.

Though their time together had been short, Collins had clearly meant something to Bishop.

Wiping her eyes, Bishop deflected, "So, what's the plan, Kasey?"

"I was going to head down to the morgue and tidy up. Collins cornered me there, and the place is still trashed, or at least it will be if Vida hasn't arrived yet. Best I take care of that before he gets in and has a heart attack. There is no way he'll take kindly to having his office turned upside down."

"That is very true," Bishop replied. "Any chance we could get your statement today?"

"Sure thing, Bishop. Just let me tidy up downstairs before Vida gets in, then I'll pop back up and we can take care of it."

"You sure it's not too soon?" Bishop asked.

"Look, the longer I avoid it, the harder it will be for me to get past it. I'll be better once I can put this whole affair behind me."

The elevator doors opened, and Kasey stepped onto the lift.

Bishop reached out her hand to stop the doors from closing. "It's good to see you on your feet, Kasey, but when we are done with your statement, you should take some time to recover. You've been through a lot."

Kasey ignored her instincts and wrapped her arms around Bishop. "I'll think about it. Thanks for having my back yesterday."

As Kasey embraced Bishop, a familiar mist descended over her vision, blotting out the lobby of the Ninth Precinct.

What the...? A vision—now?

When the mist cleared, Kasey found herself standing in an elevator, but the Ninth Precinct was nowhere to be seen.

Instead, the elevator she occupied was old and poorly maintained. Its dirty green carpet was worn through from decades of wear and tear. The doors likewise were scuffed and tarnished.

She looked down and recognized her own clothes.

It's me, she realized with a start.

She seldom experienced visions from her own life. They tended to revolve around others, sometimes an individual, and other times large swathes of people, but never had she experienced a glimpse into her own future.

She was in uncharted waters.

Looking down, she knew it was definitely her. She could clearly see her left arm still wore the bandage Vida had patched her up with after the fight at Hudson Road.

Searching for a time line, she realized her clothes were different than what she was now wearing.

At least it's not today.

She watched as the elevator's ancient readout slowly moved from the third-floor button to the second, and then to the ground floor. The elevation halted with a clunking sound.

The aluminum doors parted, revealing a long hallway. Apartment doors ran the length of the corridor.

She stepped out of the elevator.

A figure ran down the hall away from her, the pantsuit all too familiar.

Bishop!

Confused, Kasey took off down the hall after her.

She heard herself speak the words, "Hey Bishop, where did she go?"

Bishop stopped and turned to face Kasey, her demeanor cold and impassive. Without warning, she drew her Glock and pointed it at Kasey. Kasey's breath caught in her throat.

Then, as suddenly as it had begun, the vision ended. Grey mist clouded her vision like a dense fog. When it cleared, Kasey was face-to-face with Bishop, her arms still wrapped around her in a hug.

Bishop was trying to extricate herself from the awkward embrace.

"Are you sure you're alright, Kasey?" Bishop asked. "That's an awfully firm grip you've got there."

Kasey let go, trying to process what she had just witnessed. "Oh, sorry. I drifted off for a moment, my bad."

She stepped back, and the elevator doors slid shut, blocking out Detective Bishop and her look of confusion and concern.

Kasey rode the lift down to the morgue, replaying the vision in her mind. What could it have meant? Why would Bishop ever threaten her with a gun?

Entering the morgue, Kasey was met with widespread destruction. Steel trays and morgue implements were scattered across the floor. A set of shelves lay where it had fallen.

"Oh, man," Kasey said to herself. "I need to get this cleaned up before Vida gets in. He will lose his mind if he sees his morgue in this state."

Sitting in the center of the room lay a steel gurney with a large white body bag resting on it. As it hadn't been there last night, there was only one possibility.

Danilo Lelac.

She made her way over to the gurney and unzipped the heavy white plastic sheath. Instantly, she regretted it. The half-toasted remains of Danilo Lelac were an unwelcome sight.

In an effort to hide the truth of what had happened there, Kasey had almost burnt down her apartment. What none of her colleagues knew was that Collins was a Werewolf. She wanted to keep it that way.

The Werewolf was both a magical creature and part of a World that lay outside the public eye. The World of Magic relied on secrecy to guard against the superstitions and prejudices of mankind. History had not been kind to witches and wizards. Purges and persecution had always followed swiftly in the wake of discovery.

Kasey's purpose in coming to the station was to ensure that the World of Magic remained undetected. And that required destroying what little remained of Danilo's corpse. She needed to ensure no trace of the shapeshifter remained. She simply couldn't risk Vida performing an autopsy or running any samples. Not to mention how difficult it would be to explain away the cause of death.

Kasey had killed the Werewolf by stabbing him through the heart with the Spear of Odin. The ancient artifact was made entirely of silver, a substance anathema to the lupine creatures. The silver had stilled Danilo's beating heart and ended the creature's reign of bloodshed.

Unfortunately, spears are pretty hard to come by in 21st-century New York City. The wounds it had caused would be difficult to reason away. Kasey couldn't have Vida asking any more questions.

She hunted around the room for options. Hiding the body would not be sufficient; it needed to be destroyed.

I'll never be able to sneak it out of here on my own.

She began to tidy the morgue as she searched for an answer. She picked up the discarded steel trays and restored them to their place on the Morgue's examination table. Returning to the floor she gathered the scattered implements. Among them she spotted a bone saw lying on the floor where it had fallen during the fight. She looked at the saw, then to Danilo, and then back to the saw.

Ew, that's disgusting. No way I'm cutting that thing into pieces.

Hunting for other options, she spotted the incinerator. The machine was used for destroying contaminated waste, but it was far too small to deal with something the size of Danilo's body.

Kasey wracked her brain.

"I can shrink him," Kasey said, smiling at the thought.

In the Academy, she had always been cautioned against using such spells on living creatures.

"Most of them will not survive the shrinking and growing process," her professor had droned on. "The damage to the cells is too severe."

Kasey looked at the body before her and shrugged. "I'm not really worried about him surviving, so I guess it's not a problem."

Staring at the body, she envisioned the size she wished him to be. *"Crebachu!"*

She felt the power surge through her being.

An odd gurgling noise filled the morgue as the white plastic shroud and everything inside it began to shrink. In a matter of moments, the giant corpse had shrunk to the size of a matchbox car.

During his lifetime, Danilo Lelac had been almost seven feet tall, an absolute giant of a man and an even more terrifying Werewolf. Seeing him so small was almost comical.

Kasey scooped up the miniature body bag and hastily jammed it into the medical incinerator. After setting the temperature to max, she turned on the incinerator.

A faint whoosh rose from the machine as it whirred to life. Leaving it to do its work, she returned to tidying the morgue. She stooped to pick up a tray off the floor, then set it on the counter. It was still a little bent out of shape from where she had clobbered Collins with it.

Memories of the fight came flooding back but she tried to drive them away. She had no desire to revisit the experience that had almost killed her.

She preferred to focus on what lay ahead. Thinking of the vision of Bishop caused her hands to tremble. She knew Bishop would be upset about Collins, but even then, mad enough to pull a gun on her? It seemed unlikely, even for Bishop.

Kasey made a mental note to keep an eye on the detective.

Leaning on the examination table, she regathered her thoughts. More than anything, Kasey longed to know who was behind the coming attack on the city. Part of her had hoped that being near Danilo might trigger another vision, but no such luck.

It seemed the killer's body would yield no further clues, for her or for Vida. The incinerator would see to that.

Setting aside her worries with Bishop and the pending attack, she realized she still needed to deal with the Ainsleys. John's lawsuit had come out of nowhere; it seemed a foolish gambit even for the spoiled brat.

To follow through on the lawsuit, he would have to admit to harassing Kasey in open court. It really didn't make much sense. It seemed more likely than pursuing the lawsuit, he had simply moved onto the next phase in his life's mission to make her miserable.

"If I see him again, I'll wring his wretched neck," Kasey told herself.

"Wring whose neck?" a richly accented voice called from the door.

CHAPTER THREE

*K*asey spun to find Vida standing in the doorway. His mouth was agape. "Kasey, what happened to my morgue?"

In spite of her efforts, the room was still trashed. She countered with a question of her own. "You've heard about Collins, right?"

Vida nodded as he hesitantly crept into the mess. "Yeah, Bishop told me about him. It's a little creepy when you think about it, though. We were working side by side with a psycho and didn't even know it."

"Tell me about it," she replied, scooping a scalpel and some forceps off the floor and placing them in the sink. "I had no idea until he jumped me last night. Unfortunately, he picked here to do it. This was the collateral damage."

"Looks like you put up a hell of a fight," Vida replied.

"Yeah, didn't do me a lot of good, though. Still managed to knock me out and get me out of the station."

Vida set his bag down on the counter. "That's the part that doesn't make any sense to me. Why take you? He killed the others, so why not just kill you here?"

She hadn't been ready for that one and she scrambled for an answer that wouldn't reveal her gift. "I'm not sure, Vida. It seemed like he was trying to leverage me to get at the other targets. He took a risk to go after Kelly Sachs, but he must have realized that it was a one off. It wasn't going to keep working for him."

"Seems like taking you didn't work out too well for him either," Vida replied. "I heard you barbecued him. Speaking of which, where is he? They told me the body had been brought in."

She shrugged. "No idea. I only just got in myself. I figured I'd take care of some of this mess before you arrived. I was hoping to save you from having a heart attack when you saw it."

"Too late for that," Vida said. "It's odd though. I'll have to work out where that body has got to."

Fixing her gaze on the toppled shelves before her, Kasey grabbed the frame and hefted it upright. The shelves tottered off balance before falling backward—right on top of her.

Vida reached out to help but missed the mark, instead grabbing hold of her bandaged arm.

"The shelves, Vida, not me," she groaned through gritted teeth as she struggled against the weight of the steel.

"Sorry!" Releasing Kasey, he grabbed the nearest shelf and together they righted them and rolled them back against the wall.

When the shelves came to a halt, Vida clicked the wheel locks down and fastened them into place.

Turning, Vida reached for Kasey's injured arm. His face was creased with worry. "I'm so sorry, Kasey. I didn't mean to."

Kasey looked down at her arm and put two and two together.

I didn't feel a thing. Mom must have healed it with the others this morning.

"All good, Vida, don't give it another thought."

The incinerator chimed.

Oh no!

In her scrambling to cover her actions, Kasey had forgotten that feature of the machine.

"What's in the incinerator?" he asked.

"Oh, don't mind that. I was examining Lincoln Strode's body when Collins jumped me. I ended up a little closer to Strode than I had hoped, so I burned my clothes to avoid risk of infection."

He nodded approvingly. "Probably a good idea. Now that the

case is closed, we'll be doing the same thing with him. Turns out he doesn't have any family here to collect the body."

She felt for Danilo's victim. "That's awful. Being cremated by the state isn't much of a way to go out."

"Is there such a thing as a good way to go?" Vida asked as he straightened one of the autopsy tables that had been shunted out of place.

She pondered for a moment before replying, "Death due to excessive sugar consumption seems like a winner to me."

"Donuts?" he asked.

"Too cliché. I think I'd rather set a record on the way out. Something like consuming my body weight in chocolate." Kasey nodded. "Yes, that would do nicely."

"You are an odd one, Kasey, you know that?" he answered resting against the heavy steel table.

"Perhaps. I think it's simply a matter of perspective." She dusted her hands together. "Any chance you can finish up here? Most of my place was cooked last night. I still need to duck out and pick up some essentials."

"Can do," he answered.

"Thanks," she replied as she grabbed her bag off the counter and slung it over her shoulder. "If you see Bishop, let her know I'll be back for my statement."

I have something I need to return as well.

She left the morgue and opted for the stairs. After her earlier vision, she was still feeling a little hesitant about Bishop. It would be easier to avoid the detective if she didn't have to step out of an elevator in the station's lobby. Emerging from the staircase she quietly slipped out the station's side door.

Kasey did intend to go shopping, just not the variety of store Vida might have supposed. First stop was a trip to the Emporium.

The Emporium was a one stop shop for magical supplies and artifacts. Its owner, Ernesto Thompson, specialized in meeting the needs of New York City's thriving magical community.

Most importantly, Ernesto had graciously loaned Kasey the Spear of Odin that she had used to put an end to Danilo Lelac once and for all.

Forged by the Norse wizard Odin, it was the very blade he had wielded when driving the Werewolf scourge from Scandinavia. The artifact was a potent weapon, one that had been lost in the sands of time.

How Ernesto had come to possess the weapon was not quite clear. Fortunately, he had been willing to lend it to her in exchange for a small favor. In parting with the spear, he had been quite clear that it was to be returned once it was no longer needed. Not one to owe favors or accumulate debts, returning the spear was at the forefront of her to-do-list.

Kasey was also more than a little curious as to what other wonders the Emporium might hold. Her previous visit had allowed only a passing glimpse into the many marvels the store had to offer.

With the NYPD giving her time off to recover, she considered the Emporium and its inventory to be crucial research in her current undertaking.

While she had no idea who was behind the looming attack, Danilo had made it more than clear they were a fearsome foe. It seemed only common sense to presume they were part of the magical community. If that were the case, she could use any edge she could get in the fight to come.

Making her way through the streets, she breathed a sigh of relief. She loved the hustle and bustle of New York City. It was one of the reasons she had wanted to live here. No matter where and when one might venture outside, there was always something going on. Kasey's childhood had been lonely, thanks to her gift, but in New York City, she was never alone.

"Why would anyone want to destroy this?" she asked, thinking of the vision she had witnessed. She had watched in terror as widespread destruction was unleashed across the city. The towering skyscrapers that were the pride of New York had cracked and ultimately crumbled in the face of the attack.

Kasey remembered the terror she had felt as building after building collapsed. Screaming had filled the air as her vision had cut off.

She was determined to do everything she could to prevent such carnage befalling the city.

For a moment, she considered telling the Arcane Council, but her mother's warning rang in her ears. Perhaps Jane was just being a little paranoid about the council. After all, the Stonemoores had more reason than most to be concerned. More than once in their family history they had suffered great tragedy, not only at the hands of non-magical beings. At times, they had also suffered due to the shifting sands of changing governments in the magical community.

For the time being, I'll keep it to myself.

She arrived at the Emporium, or at least its street front facade. The Museum of Reclaimed Urban Space, or MORUS, was a convenient disguise for the enormous store. The tours that the museum operated accounted for the steady flow of traffic. Seldom did such an old and neglected part of New York City attract unwanted attention but when it did the museum was the perfect cover.

The surrounding tenements had been the scene of the lengthy dispute between the city and the squatters who had taken up residence there. Ernesto's family had brokered a treaty between them and in thanks, the city had gifted the building known as C squat to the Thompsons.

C squat itself was quite modest but Ernesto and his family had a grand vision. Located deep beneath the Earth, the Emporium had expanded considerably. No longer the simple basement it has once been. Its aisles now ran for miles underneath the city that never slept. Ernesto boasted that anything a wizard might ever want could be found within its walls and in Kasey's experience, the claim was well founded.

She walked through the door to find a woman standing in a white shirt and pleated blue skirt. The sign beside her now read, 'Museum of Reclaimed Urban Space. Next tour 9:30'.

The woman in the tour guide uniform smiled at her. "Hello and welcome to the Museum of Reclaimed Urban Space. Are you here for the tour?"

Following her sister's example from their previous visit, Kasey replied, "No, thank you, I'm here for the gift store."

The woman pointed to the hall at the back of the store. "I take it you know the way?"

"Sure do," Kasey replied

"Then head on through, I hope you find what you're looking for."

Kasey returned the woman's smile and thanked her. Making her way through the small tour station, she found the hallway leading to the restrooms. The cupboard labeled cleaning stood to the right. Kasey grabbed the door handle and opened it. Learning from her previous experience, she flicked on the light and closed the door behind her.

"Disgyn."

The lift rocketed downward, but this time Kasey was ready. Holding onto a shelf for support, she enjoyed the swift descent.

As the lift slowed, a familiar purple light appeared in the air before her. The light raced back and forward as if controlled by an unseen hand, spelling out the word, 'Welcome'.

She opened the door and was greeted by the opulent foyer of the Emporium.

She couldn't help but smile. Something about the place simply excited her.

She headed over to the information counter. Ernesto was behind the counter, scribbling on a piece of paper. He looked up as she approached.

"Kasey!" he called. "It is wonderful to see you again"

She came to a halt by the counter. "Ernesto, it's good to see you too."

"After your recent visit, I wasn't expecting to see you so soon," he said as he made his way around the counter.

She smiled. "Me neither. Fortunately, my situation resolved itself much sooner than expected, and ended far better than I had hoped, thanks to you."

He leaned closer so that he could not be overheard. "Miss Stonemoore, am I to believe that you triumphed over the infamous Danilo Lelac in less than a day?"

She nodded. "I would have died if it wasn't for your help. I threw everything I had at him and he just about killed me and destroyed my apartment, but at the end of the day, it was the Spear of Odin that put him down for good. The spear saved my life. You saved my life, Ernesto."

Ernesto blushed. "It's the least I could do, Miss Stonemoore. Werewolves killing young women in New York, it's uncivilized and I won't stand for it. I am so glad to see that you are safe. Will you be requiring the spear further?"

She shook her head. "No, thanks, Ernesto. I'm pretty sure there was only one rampaging Werewolf out to kill me. I know the spear is valuable, so I wanted to get it back here safely as soon as I could."

Kasey reached into her pocket and fished out the shard. The potent weapon had been a great comfort to her during the ordeal with Danilo. She almost didn't want to part with it but something about the weapon also unsettled her. Gingerly, she handed the gleaming artifact to Ernesto.

As soon as the artifact left her hand, she felt lighter. It was as if a weight had been lifted off her shoulders.

Ernesto took the sliver with a flourish and tucked it into his suit coat. "I'll ensure that it makes its way back to the vault, Miss Stonemoore. If you ever need it again, you know where to find it."

Kasey nodded as the strange sensation of relief washed over her entire being. She couldn't help but smile as the dark cloud that had followed her since she had killed Danilo dispersed.

Initially, she had thought it was a misplaced sense of guilt over taking another's life, even in self-defense. Now she felt it might be something else.

Ernesto gave a knowing smile. "That sensation is no coincidence, Miss Stonemoore. I have felt it myself. One cannot wield the Spear of Odin without bearing the weight of its legacy upon their shoulders."

"I don't understand," Kasey said. "What was that? And why is it gone?"

"All power comes with a price, and the Spear of Odin is no exception. Countless lives have ended on its blade. Odin is said to have forged it from silver and the tears of his own sorrow at the loss of his family. Whatever the truth is, those who take a life with it, soon feel the weight of the blade's bloody legacy."

"So, you have felt it then?" she asked.

"Of course. As I've said before, knowledge is power, and I do not speak from ignorance when I talk of the blade. There is a reason it is hidden in the vault and not carried with me every day."

She nodded empathetically. Knowing Ernesto had taken a life

with the spear changed Kasey's opinion of him. Clearly, there was more to Ernesto than she had realized.

"Miss Stonemoore, I don't suppose you have had an opportunity to speak with your father?" he asked.

"Indeed, I have," she replied. "I stayed with my parents last night. He laughed when I had mentioned the box but told me he would take your offer into consideration. Tell me Ernesto, what is inside it?"

"You will have to ask him," Ernesto answered, straightening up to his full height. As he adjusted the fall of his suit, he smiled. "Some secrets are not mine to share. I appreciate you keeping your word. Is there anything else I can help you with, Miss Stonemoore?"

"I was just going to take a look around," she replied. "Most of my wardrobe was wiped out in the fight that killed Danilo. I don't suppose you sell any ordinary clothes here?"

Ernesto looked Kasey up and down. "I wouldn't say I sell ordinary clothes, no..." As Kasey's face fell, he continued. "But I do have a range of exceptional attire for any occasion. What are you looking for? Something to wear out and about, or are you like the other young hopefuls? Looking for something nice for this evening's gala?"

"Gala?" she asked. "What Gala?"

"Why, the Met Gala, of course," Ernesto replied producing a measuring tape from his suit pocket. "Anyone who is anyone will be there."

Kasey's mind turned to her Ainsley problem and the pending lawsuit. "When you say anyone, what are the chances that Counselor Ainsley will be in attendance?"

"Arthur?" Ernesto laughed as he began to take Kasey's measurements. "Most certainly. The counselor hasn't missed one in years. He and the mayor are good friends. I imagine others of the council will be there also. In a city like New York, the influence of the Arcane Council and that of governmental bureaucracy run along the same lines."

"Money," Kasey replied.

"Precisely," Ernesto answered, drawing the tape around Kasey's waist. "I don't suppose you've been invited?"

Kasey thought back to her agreement with Arthur Ainsley. The counsellor had promised her that in exchange for dealing with Danilo discreetly, he would ensure John left her in peace. John's lawsuit was a flagrant violation of their agreement, Kasey intended to hold him to his word. The gala was her best chance for a face-to-face meeting.

Nodding she answered. "In a manner of speaking, Ernesto. In a manner of speaking."

The proprietor raised an eyebrow, but Kasey spared him further concern.

"Now, Ernesto, I can't be going to the gala in these old rags. Care to show me what you've got that would be more suitable?"

Ernesto offered his arm. "Why, of course, Miss Stonemoore. Let me show you to our evening wear. I'm sure you'll find that no mundane tailor can match our magical ministrations."

Ernesto guided her through the emporium and down an aisle labelled 'Formal Wear'. Ernesto stopped halfway down the aisle and began flicking through the garments that were hanging there.

"I know it's here somewhere," Ernesto mused, moving along the row.

"Aha!" he hoisted a hangar into the air. A silver evening gown hung neatly from it.

Kasey took in the dress. It certainly looked the part. "May I?" Kasey asked.

"Of course," Ernesto answered, handing over the dress.

Kasey held the gown in front of her and walked over to a mirror to check her reflection.

Damn. That does look good. Kasey admitted to herself.

Seeing a price tag dangling from the hangar, she turned it over, so that she could read it.

"Wow. It's beautiful but I don't think I can afford it."

Ernesto laughed. "I'm sure that I can do something about the price, but at the end of the day. Some things are worth it Kasey. Pay peanuts, get monkeys. That's what my father always said."

Kasey eyed the dress. *I guess a little retail therapy to deal with the stress of the past week won't hurt.*

"Will it last, Ernesto? I can't have it falling apart before I've paid off the card," she had said as she gawked at the price tag, "and based on the tag that will be sometime around Christmas."

His mouth peaked into a smile. "Miss Stonemoore, I assure you this garment will outlast anything else you own. I picked it not only because I thought you'd look fabulous in it, which you do, but also you might find its other properties useful, given your history."

"Other properties? Like what?" Kasey had asked.

"Oh no, Miss Stonemoore, I wouldn't deprive you of the joys of discovering them for yourself."

"I'll take it," Kasey answered. "I don't suppose you've got some heels that would match?"

Ernesto glanced down the aisle. "Oh, I'm sure I could find something that would suit. If you could hand me the dress, I'll have our tailors adjust the fit for you."

Kasey surrendered the dress, "How long will that take?"

"Minutes Kasey, mere minutes. Their magic does wonders, even on a tight schedule. Take a seat on the lounge there, I'll be back in a moment."

As Ernesto disappeared down the aisle dress in hand, Kasey turned her mind to the gala and her last remaining hurdle. Her invitation, or lack thereof.

It's only a museum, how hard can it be to break into?

CHAPTER FOUR

*A*ll around Kasey, cameras flashed like a disco strobe light as she made her way down 5th Avenue. A veritable sea of paparazzi surged around the entryway of the Metropolitan Museum of Art, or the Met as it was known around the world, held in check only by a cordon of bollards, barriers, and towering security guards.

Ernesto hadn't been lying when he'd said the Gala was the social event of the year. She watched awestruck as the recent winner of American Divas got out of her limousine and was ushered toward the front door by her security detail. Her security parted like the Red Sea as she did a quick turn on the Red Carpet, allowing the hungry press to snap a few photos before she disappeared through the front doors.

The luxury cars formed a motorcade stretching around the block and, one by one, New York's elite made their way into the exclusive Gala.

She eyed the front door.

That's never going to work.

Magic or not, there would be no fooling the press of paparazzi and the throng of gossip reporters that formed a gauntlet between her and the door.

"Plan B it is!" Kasey resolved as she turned and made her way around the museum toward Central Park. Reaching the park, the scent of freshly mown grass wafted into her nostrils.

Entering the park, Kasey passed a man in his thirties who was out for his evening jog. She caught his eye, and they lingered. Ernesto had delivered once more, and Kasey was killing it. The slinky silver evening dress shone like quicksilver as it moved with her every step. A split ran up to her right thigh, enough to tease but more importantly, gave her freedom to move. Or, at least it would have if not for the stunning silver heels she had paired with the dress.

The ensemble had maxed out her credit card but as she examined herself now she decided the price tag was well and truly worth it.

As Kasey made her way around the Met, the security cordon lessened but there were still regular guards stationed around the museum's exterior.

Reaching the building's southern corner, she found what she was looking for: a section of wall where the greenery of Central Park ran right up to the museum.

Now I just need to get to the wall unseen.

Only one thing stood in her way: a glowering security guard.

Standing just off the path, the guard had his arms folded across his broad chest. He scanned the park. Kasey considered trying a more direct approach by charming her way past the guard. As much as she knew she was rocking her dress, she considered herself a clumsy flirt at the best of times and she was out of practice.

"Better to play to my strengths, break and entry it is," she whispered to herself. Bending down, she untied the straps on her heels while she waited, making as if they were too loose. She didn't need to wait long as a cyclist soon appeared, cruising along the path behind the museum. When the cyclist reached the security guard, Kasey whispered her incantation. "*Egwyl.*"

The cyclist's wheel shot off its frame. Kasey's spell had shattered the aluminum fitting securing his wheel to his bike. The front fork of the bicycle plowed into the sidewalk, throwing the poor cyclist over the handlebars. He slammed into the waiting security guard.

Kasey felt awful, but she needed the distraction. As the two collapsed in a heap, Kasey slipped off her heels, picked them up, and sprinted across the grass. She ducked into the foliage.

Holding her breath, she peered out to ensure no one had paid attention to her mad dash. The security guard was still locked in a heated argument with the cyclist who was apologizing profusely. No one else was around.

Content she was unobserved, she focused on the museum wall before her. "*Llwybr.*"

The concrete shimmered as magic pulsed through the normally inert stone. Soon, a seam appeared in the wall. It ran from the foundation straight up to a point just above Kasey's head. Slowly, the seam parted, and the concrete peeled back.

Kasey continued to focus on the wall before her. The concrete was far thicker than she had anticipated and a trickle of sweat ran down her brow as the spell drained her strength.

Suddenly, a sliver of light glimmered through the gap. It was small, but it gave her hope. She gave the spell more energy. Soon, the hole was just large enough she could squeeze through. On the other side, she released her incantation. The concrete surged closed before resuming its solid form.

She turned to take in her surroundings. She had entered into one of the Met's many exhibition halls.

The room was dark, the only light originating from a neon green exit sign above a doorway leading to the next room. The centerpiece of the gala was the fashion exhibit that was on display in the museum's Central Exhibition Gallery. The rest of the museum appeared to have been closed off to keep the guests out of trouble.

Kasey slid back into her heels and smoothed her dress, then took care to pick the leaves out of her hair. She couldn't help but feel self-conscious as she tended to her appearance. She had never been to the gala, most people on Earth hadn't for that matter. The Met Gala was reserved for the famous, the wealthy, and the elite.

Now that she was inside, she needed to find Arthur Ainsley without causing too much of a stir. The Chairman of the Arcane Council may have been able to duck her calls, but he couldn't avoid her in the middle of an exhibition hall. She would see to that. Working her way toward the gala, she simply hoped that invitations were only checked at the door.

She crossed the hall and turned into a corridor. Following the sound of the gala, she made her way through the darkened museum and emerged in a room full of European sculptures. She admired a particularly impressive cast of Rodin's The Thinker.

"Hey, you there. What are you doing in here? The Museum's closed."

Kasey turned to find a security guard walking toward her. Racing to construct an alibi, Kasey pretended to be searching the hall intently.

"I said, what are you doing here? The gala is in the central hall."

Kasey turned to face the guard. "I'm sorry, I'm looking for my husband. He's disappeared and, well, there was a blonde waitress, that was giving him a little too much attention. I don't mean to be suspicious but..."

The guard gave a knowing nod. "Be that as it may, we can't have you wandering about in the dark. Head back to the gala. I'll keep an eye out for anyone dallying out here. He's probably just in the bathroom, you know. Don't be so quick to think the worst."

Kasey nodded sheepishly. "I guess you're right, thanks."

The guard pointed down the hall. "Head on in. I have to finish my rounds."

Kasey's heels clicked against the tiles as she strode for the central exhibit. The door leading to the central exhibit was open, and she made her way into the gala.

She halted in the doorway. "Wow."

The central exhibition theater had been transformed into an exquisite winter wonderland. Elegant ice sculptures towered over the assembled elite. Rows of tables lined the outer edge while a raised runway ran down the center of the hall. Waiters bustled to and from the kitchen, ferrying trays of hors d'oeuvres and champagne to the guests.

Kasey stared in awe at an immense ice-castle that ran the length of one wall. Each brick was carefully hewn to shape and fitted together, forming the masterpiece. She was so enamored with the grandeur of the hall that she missed the patron standing before her. Tripping over their foot, Kasey stumbled forward.

"Oh," she cried as she fell forward into another guest. Kasey grabbed the only thing within reach that she could find, his outstretched arm.

Latching hold of his arm with both of hers, she steadied herself.

"I'm so sorry, these stupid heels." She looked up, then her apologetic smile twisted into anger. "You!"

It took a moment for John Ainsley to recognize her. The slinky silver dress was a far cry from her usual day at the OCME. "Kasey?"

She let go of his arm and squared up to the man who had made her life a misery.

"Come now, Kasey, surely you're not going to hit me again in a room full of witnesses?"

Kasey seethed, clenching and unclenching her fists as she considered doing exactly that. Over the course of the last week, she had thought of what she'd do to John if she came face-to-face with him again.

His lawsuit was just the latest in a string of irritations that had been wearing on her nerves.

"Come to think of it, Kasey, what are you doing here? You don't seem to be with anyone and I know you didn't get an invite on your own. So..."

"So, what, John? Unless there was a restraining order in those papers you served me, it's none of your damn business. Now get out of my way," she replied as she gathered her things and jammed her phone back into her purse.

"Oh, so you got those?" John asked, nodding. "I was wondering if you had. Our lawyers hadn't heard anything yet, so I was curious."

"Well, John," she replied, leaning close so she could not be heard. "It just so happens that I've been a little busy. Irritating as you are, you are far from my most pressing concern."

John laughed. "Oh, come now, Kasey. I find that difficult to believe. The lawsuit was just my little way of reminding you I'm still here. You might think of me as a pain in your ass, but at least you are thinking of me."

"I wouldn't talk about my ass, John. It brings up all kinds of memories."

"I'll bet..." John replied cockily.

She fought the urge to choke him with his bow tie. Instead, she lowered her voice to a whisper. "If you haven't heard yet, last night I killed Danilo Lelac with my bare hands. Just remember I could snap your little chicken neck before anyone here could raise a finger to save you."

"Perhaps, but back at the OCME, I thought you were a normal. One of them," he almost hissed as he gestured to the room. "Now I know better. Father mentioned you were a witch. Using magic on a member of the magical community would be a matter tried in our courts. Presided over by the Arcane Council. I could kill you with a word. After our history, it would probably be classed as self-defense and thrown out before our lawyers even entered the room. I wouldn't spend a night in jail."

"Then do it." Kasey glanced at the assembled crowd. When Ainsley didn't move, she laughed. "Yeah, that room full of witnesses, huh? I didn't think so. Maybe next time."

She turned to leave, but John caught her hand. "We both know you're here without an invite, Kasey. So, stay with me, as my guest, and you can enjoy the gala."

"Stay with you? Like a date? I'd rather die," she answered.

"Come now, Kasey, that's harsh even for you."

"Harsh? John, is it really? You got me booted from the OCME, you put pressure on the NYPD, and now you are suing me for an injury resulting from an incident you yourself instigated. If we weren't in a crowded room, I'd seriously consider finishing what I started at the OCME."

John looked down at the carpet.

Kasey pressed on. "Besides what sort of message would I be sending if I let you blackmail me into a date?"

She watched as John weighed her words carefully. She stared at her former colleague as she waited for his usual witty retort.

"I get it, Kasey. I've been an ass," John struggled to say.

Kasey's face scrunched in confusion. The admission had caught her flat-footed, while the understatement brought her blood to the boil.

"An ass? You've almost ruined my life. It took me years to get to the OCME and you managed to screw everything up in an afternoon."

His shoulders sank. "I'm sorry, Kasey. I know an apology doesn't mean much now, but I'll make it all the same. I'll have the suit dropped and call off the dogs. I'll also speak with the OCME and get you your old job back if you want it."

Kasey was skeptical. "What's the catch? You want me to be your date for the evening?"

John shook his head. "No. You're right, I've done enough already. There is no catch and no conditions. I should have done it weeks ago. I guess I just wanted your attention and went about it the wrong way. Enjoy the party, Kasey. Take care that you aren't caught though. These folks are snobs even by my standards. They will press charges if you are caught."

He paused awkwardly, like he had more something to say.

Kasey had never seen this side of him.

Whatever he might have been thinking, he thought better of it. "Have a good night, Kasey."

He turned to walk away.

She thought about John's warning. If anyone stopped her, her story would fall apart like a wet paper bag. Besides, she'd come to the gala to get the lawsuit dropped and if John was true to his word, it would be. She was tired of the uncertainty though and her best opportunity for making sure it happened was right in front of her. She ground her teeth as she weighed her choices.

I can't believe I'm even considering this, but I've bought this dress. I may as well enjoy the gala.

She silenced her inner critic.

"Hey, John, wait up," she called.

He halted, looking back at her.

"Care to show me around?"

John smiled. It was different this time, not at all the cocky grin she'd become accustomed to.

"Sure," he exclaimed, holding out his arm for her to take.

She eyed the arm and shook her head, "Baby steps John."

"Of course," he said, motioning to the fashion on display. "Have you seen this year's exhibit?"

Kasey shook her head. "No, I haven't had the chance yet."

"Oh, you must see it," he said. "It's like nothing a real person would ever actually wear in the snow. It's fantastic."

"Lead the way," she replied.

"Sure. Oh, let me introduce you to a few people." He pointed to a group of patrons near the exhibit. "Over there on the left is Senator Abrams. Thomas may be a Democrat, but more importantly, he's one of ours."

"One of ours?" Kasey repeated.

"A wizard," John whispered. "Holding one of the highest offices in the land." He waved at the gray-haired senator. "Hey, Thomas, I have someone I'd like you to meet."

Thomas excused himself from the group he was speaking to and sauntered toward John.

A piercing scream split the room.

Kasey turned to see a flood of movement at the door as the sound of a submachine gun split the air.

CHAPTER FIVE

O ne of the room's ornate chandeliers came crashing to the floor. Glass scattered in every direction.

There was a shrieking stampede as the gala's guests tried to flee from the gunfire.

A dozen assailants, all dressed identically in black from head to toe, streamed into the hall. Their only distinguishing feature were their masks, each bore a caricature of a famous historical figure.

Kasey glanced at the rear entrance she had used. Three more assailants had taken position in front of it.

They each carried the same weapon, Heckler and Koch MP5 submachine guns. She couldn't help but feel bothered at the sensation of being killed by the likes of cartooned Abraham Lincoln and Thomas Jefferson.

The patrons fled before the intruders only to find others blocking their path.

As one, the surging mass of patrons retreated toward the immense ice sculpture that ran along the wall of the exhibit.

A voice rang out through the hall. It carried over the noise like a ringleader at the circus. "Ladies and gentlemen of New York City. Welcome to this evening's main event. We are so glad that you could all join us, and we are even more thrilled that you have turned out in your finest attire."

The voice was coming from the southern end of the hall, the main entrance.

Kasey strove for a better view. One of the masked intruders advanced on the guests. His movements were confident and self-assured. He held his submachine gun at the ready. In spite of his short stature, his powerful voice commanded attention. Over his face he wore a caricature of the Mongol warlord Genghis Khan.

"As you are no doubt beginning to wonder, this is a robbery," he announced. "You may call me the Khan. It is as good a name as any, I suppose."

The Khan raised his gloved hand in a closed fist. Extending one finger, he waggled it before the room. "I must inform you that this evening, while we intend to rob you blind, we have no intention of you being harmed in the process."

Kasey stumbled as one of the gala guests backed into her. Steadying herself, she considered kicking off the silver stilettos but didn't want to draw any undue attention.

The Khan continued pointing to the entryway. "If you follow our instructions, you will all remain as healthy as the moment you walked through those doors." He paused before continuing. "Should you disobey our directions, we will have no choice but to make an example of you.

"We're more than aware that this event is well attended by New York's finest, doubtless accompanied by your personal security. Before any of you are stupid enough to draw your weapons, you should consider the following.

"One, you are outgunned. Whatever concealed weapons you are carrying, they are no match for an MP5.

"Second, know that a number of our party have brought along a little surprise." The Khan opened his jacket as he spoke, revealing a vest covered in pouches and wires.

Kasey's heart went into overdrive, it was beating so fast it threatened to leap out of her chest.

"We're carrying enough C4 to turn everyone in this room into a fine red mist. It will likely also bring down the roof of this historic structure, and none of us want that. So, for the sake of this fine museum, and your lives, I must insist that none of you make any sudden or foolish moves," the Khan continued.

"Our vests are rigged with dead men switches. Should anything happen to us, they will detonate, as will a number of other charges that we have set around the museum.

"We would much rather be considered thieves than murderers, so I must request that you follow our instructions to the letter."

More than a dozen of the armed men stood in the exhibition hall, corralling the gala guests, forcing them away from the safety of the doors and the halls that lay beyond.

There was a flurry of movement to her right: the pop super-star she had seen emerging from her limousine earlier. Her previous confidence was now gone, and a look of abject terror had replaced it. The star hid huddled behind her private security.

The security guard looked at the Khan advancing. Glancing behind him at the wall, he must have realized they were running out of room. He reached inside his suit coat and drew a pistol.

Before the security guard could raise the weapon, the Khan's submachine gun answered the threat.

The shots hammered into the security guard's chest. He dropped like a rock. The diva screamed and forced her way deeper into the safety of the crowd.

As one, the guests backed away from the fallen guard fearful that in proximity to him they might be next to draw the wrath of the Khan.

The Khan approached the guard who was lying on the floor. He cocked his head.

Kasey looked closer. *Wait, there is no blood.*

"Oh, you are wearing a vest. That was lucky for you. I promise the next one will bring some sense into that thick skull of yours. Draw a weapon again and I will kill you."

The Khan picked up the pistol off the ground and tucked it into the back of his pants "I think I'll keep this one just in case. I wouldn't want anyone else getting any foolish ideas."

Addressing the crowd, the Khan continued. "Ladies and gentlemen, I'm going to need you to form a line against the wall. Step behind the tables there.

"Keep your hands where we can see them at all times. If we see any of you using a phone, be it a text a tweet or a phone call, rest assured we'll kill you.

"If the police show up, there will be a shootout and spoiler alert, many of you will also die. So, it is in your best interest to cooperate so that we may leave, and you can resume enjoying the remainder of your evening."

The Khan addressed the cowering patrons. "Now I must insist that we relieve you of any jewelry or other items of value in your possession. In case your perception of value differs from mine, value includes: your wallets, watches, and jewelry. You can keep your expensive threads though. We aren't barbarians.

"Now if you could remove your personal effects and hand them to my companion Shakespeare. He will collect them, and we will be on our way. Does anyone have any questions?"

No one was bold enough to say a word. The man that had been identified as Shakespeare advanced toward the group.

"Get behind the tables and line up!" The Khan demanded.

The gala patrons filed through the tables and began to form a long line running parallel with the wall.

Shakespeare released his grip on his weapon. The MP5 dangled in front of his chest, suspended by a leather strap that ran over his shoulder. With his hands free, he pulled from his backpack a large black sack and made his way to the end of the line.

"You heard the Khan, folks. Wallets, watches, and jewelry. Toss 'em in the bag and no one gets hurt."

Kasey shuffled backward disturbing a patron. Turning, she found herself eye level with a man's chest. Surprised, she looked up into the face of Arthur Ainsley.

Arthur looked past Kasey as he addressed John. "Son, are you alright?"

"As good as can be expected, given the circumstances," John whispered back.

"Well, Miss Chase, fancy seeing you here. To what do I owe the pleasure?" Arthur asked quietly.

"I came to speak about our deal, Arthur," Kasey glanced at John as she spoke, "but it seems that may no longer be necessary."

"Glad to hear it. We have more pressing matters at hand," he answered, turning his attention back toward the assailants.

At the Khan's direction, several gunmen disappeared back into the museum.

Shakespeare continued working his way down the line of patrons.

The guests greeted him with mixed responses. Some trembled as they handed over their wallets, necklaces, or earrings. Others wept as their nerves frayed from the tension in the hall.

Shakespeare came to a stop in front of an older woman in a striking scarlet gown. Her long blonde hair had a tinge of silver running through it. In spite of her current circumstances, the woman seemed defiant.

Shakespeare pointed at her hand. "The ring too, ma'am."

The woman shook her head. "No. This was given to me by my late husband and I will not part with it. The earrings are worth far more, and you already have those. Take them and be on your way."

Shakespeare leaned forward. "There is no room for negotiation here. ma'am. Put the ring in the bag or you'll be joining your husband in the afterlife."

The woman shook her head. Kasey could see the determination etched into her face. The ring wasn't going anywhere.

Beside the woman, her security guards bristled.

Obviously sensing the rising danger, one of them turned to her. "Mrs. Cardston, we can always get you another ring, but there's no bringing you back."

The woman didn't budge. "No, Stanley, I was married with this ring, and if this young thug wants it, he is going to have to take it off my cold dead body."

Kasey couldn't help but admire the woman's grit. From her position, she could see Stanley's left arm slowly moving behind his back and she knew what was coming.

If Shakespeare made a move, there would be bloodshed.

Around the room others seemed to sense it also. The Khan watched patiently as the exchange played out before him.

Kasey's keen observational skills allowed her to notice the subtle movements as the other security guards in the room weighed their chance of survival.

Even if they cooperated, there was never any guarantee that they would walk out of the room alive. A promise from armed thieves was hardly something one could stake their life on.

The situation was deteriorating but Kasey was at a loss as to how to stop it. There were far too many bystanders to use her magic unobserved.

Her heart pounded as a trickle of sweat ran down her face. She knew what was coming next. Not because she'd seen it in a vision, but because she could feel it in the room.

The tension in the exhibition theater rested on a knife blade and even the smallest nudge would see it descend into chaos and bloodshed.

Discovery as a witch versus death at the thieves' hands. Should it come to it, Kasey was determined to do her part, knowing her magic might make all the difference in saving lives.

Behind her back, she opened her palm and began to focus her thoughts on the armed thieves before her. As her power gathered she felt a firm hand on her shoulder.

Turning, she found Arthur Ainsley staring down at her.

"Don't you dare," he whispered. "When will you learn Kasey? Your choices will damn us all."

CHAPTER SIX

*A*rthur Ainsley towered over Kasey. His voice was quiet but unyielding. "I mean it, Miss Chase. We have an entire hall full of witnesses here. You will not expose our entire community just to save a few pieces of petty jewelry. It's just not worth it."

"It's not just jewelry, Arthur. There are lives at stake here. Can't you see it? This place is about to blow, and when it does, people are going to die."

She felt time in the room slow to a crawl. She almost expected to see a vision, but nothing came.

Shakespeare shook his outstretched hand at Mrs. Cardston. "Last chance. Give me the ring!"

The woman shook her head.

Shakespeare had had enough, he reached for his MP-5. "I told you already, this is not a negotiation."

Before Shakespeare could raise his weapon, Stanley had his gun in hand.

At point blank range, there was no chance of missing. The pistol bucked twice. It was lights out for Shakespeare as he collapsed in a heap. His bulletproof vest did him little good; Stanley had shot him through his mask.

The room exploded into a symphony of motion and chaos.

The assailants raised their weapons but hesitated. Clearly, they had expected the robbery to proceed without bloodshed.

"Everybody down!" a voice shouted from amid the hostages.

The patron's security drew their weapons.

Stanley stepped in front of his employer and unleashed a hail of bullets toward the nearest assailant.

The Khan looked from his fallen comrade, Shakespeare, to Stanley and shook his head.

"No. No. No." He raised his weapon and returned fire.

Stanley collapsed in a heap as the submachine gun stitched a line of bullets across his chest.

The gala's guests screamed. Some threw themselves on the floor and crawled toward the cover of the tables. Several of them upended tables to act as a makeshift barrier between them and the assailants.

The assailants began to fall back, guns raised and firing at anyone who lifted their heads above the cover provided by the tables.

At first glance, Kasey had supposed the thieves to be ex-military types. That prediction was proving true as the thieves lit up the room with their weapons.

The MP-5 was a popular weapon among special forces units. Swat teams continued to employ them as their preferred firearm.

To Kasey's great surprise, the suicide vests didn't detonate. She didn't have the time to give it much thought. Without immediate action, they would all die anyway. She simply hoped it was a bluff as she ducked behind a nearby table. Risking a look over her shoulder, she spotted Arthur.

He stood seemingly un-phased by the chaos unfolding around him. She squinted at him.

Perhaps he has some sort of protective artifact or relic.

He just stared straight back at her. "You leave this to us, Miss Chase. Half the Council are in this room and we have a lifetime of using our gifts unobserved. We need to ensure whatever happens that those vests don't explode. You tend to the wounded, we'll see to these thugs."

Patrons scurried everywhere as they sought simultaneously to avoid the gunfire and get out of the exhibition hall. More tables were upturned in an effort to widen the defensive barrier.

Kasey's sweeping gaze caught a cluster of guests that were still standing where they had been in the line. While other patrons cowered and did everything they could to get out of the line of fire, this group seemed rooted to the spot.

Fear. She'd felt it at Hudson Road when death had reared its jaws wide open, ready to claim her.

It wasn't that the guests didn't want to move. They simply couldn't. They were terrified, and they were sitting ducks.

Kasey forgot about herself. Kicking off her heels so she could move freely, she sprinted at the group. Time was of the essence and she couldn't afford to try to reason with them.

A bullet clipped one of the men in the shoulder. The man went down. The woman next to him screamed. Kasey crash-tackled the remaining guests to the ground to get them out of the line of fire.

The private security forces fired back. Two more assailants went down as a veritable hail of gunfire erupted from the cover of the upturned tables.

The thieves returned fire indiscriminately, causing chaos and carnage among the gala's guests.

Kasey made her way back to the upturned tables to help the security forces against the thieves.

Against Arthur's wishes, she gestured over the table and whispered the words of a spell beneath her breath.

"Dinistrio."

The arcane force struck the cluster of chairs and tables that two of the thieves were hiding behind. The furniture shredded as the energy blasted through it. The two thieves fell in a storm of deadly splinters.

Kasey breathed a sigh of relief. Her relief was short-lived when a third thief, wearing an Elvis mask appeared. He bore down on her with his gun raised. In the chaos, the thieves had made their way behind the tables and flanked the guests. Elvis now had a clear line of fire; he had her dead to rights.

Too late.

His trigger finger tightened. Kasey closed her eyes and waited for the end.

There was a faint metallic click. Nothing happened. She opened her eyes and looked at the shooter.

Elvis looked down in confusion, checking the firing mechanism before raising the gun again. He pulled the trigger a second time. Still nothing but a hollow click emanated from the weapon.

Kasey glanced over her shoulder. John Ainsley remained in his spot, a satisfied grin on his face. Clearly, John had opted for a subtle spell.

Kasey charged Elvis before the incantation could wear off. The shooter looked up. Before he could react, she collided with him and tackled him to the ground.

The thief struggled to dislodge Kasey. Wrapping herself around him, she applied pressure to his windpipe. Slowly but surely, she tightened her sleeper hold.

The thief struggled violently but it only served to hasten his fate. After a few moments that felt like an eternity, he went limp, the oxygen deprivation having rendered him unconscious.

"Elvis has left the building."

Kasey looked up to find John standing over her, a chair raised ready to club the thief.

John looked down at her still entwined with the thief and laughed. "I know he's unconscious, but is it wrong that I feel a little jealous?"

"Watch out, John," she said. "Any more of that and you join him."

She rolled the thief off her and ripped his gun away from him. Handing it to one of the nearby private security guards, she shouted, "The back door is clear. Take this and get the patrons out of here as quick as you can."

The guests didn't need to be told twice; they darted for the door.

At the exhibition hall's main entrance, the Khan and his remaining thieves fell back in disarray. Seeing the numbers turn in their favor the security forces pressed forward.

The closest thief, Abraham Lincoln dropped. His bulletproof vest stopped the first few rounds, but his unprotected legs fared worse. Unable to support his weight, his wounded legs gave out.

The Khan glanced around the room before taking one last look at the fallen Lincoln. Shaking his head, he fled through the open door, Thomas Jefferson at his side.

Searching the vast exhibition hall, Kasey pondered on her next move. Dozens of patrons lay on the floor injured. Others fled in panic. Waiters and waitresses were scattered among them. Kasey couldn't help but appreciate that in this moment of mayhem, whether one was a millionaire or barely making ends meet, it didn't matter, bullets don't show any favor to the one percent.

In the center of the hall, a wounded John F. Kennedy tried to get up off the floor.

The security forces weren't gentle. The thief went down in a hail of fire, this time for good.

With all the thieves in the room down and the remaining two on the run, the danger in the exhibition hall seemed at an end. Kasey considered chasing after the fleeing Khan but thought better of it. Scanning the hall, she realized there were many others far more suited for that task.

Members of the security details checked on their charges. One party secured the front doors to ensure the Khan could not return. Patrons fled through the hall's rear doors.

Sirens wailed in the distance.

The police would pick up the Khan soon enough.

Kasey had more pressing issues that needed her attention. What the gala's patrons needed more than anything was a doctor. And while Kasey wasn't a GP she was as close to one as the wounded patrons were going to get for the next few minutes.

Kasey set about doing triage. Running to one of the upturned tables, Kasey gathered as many of the cotton table napkins as she could find. Kasey approaching one of the injured patrons. The man had suffered a gunshot wound to his chest.

Kasey pressed a wad of napkins against the man's chest and then placed his hand over it.

"You'll need to keep the pressure on to slow the bleeding. Don't worry help will be here soon."

Turning to John, Kasey shouted. "If we can keep these people alive until the ambulance arrives, they have a chance,"

John nodded and raised his voice above the chaos, addressing those still in the room, "if you are not injured, head out the rear doors and keep going until you reach the museum's exit. If any of your party have been wounded, help us find them so that we can help."

Kasey made her way over to Stanley. His courage had started the entire stampede. She didn't need to give a thorough examination to know he was already dead. Cut down by the MP-5, he hadn't stood a chance. Kasey checked his pulse just to be sure, anyway.

Shaking her head, she moved on to the next victim. The first, a man crouched over Stanley, was bleeding from his upper arm.

"Are you hit anywhere else?" Kasey asked.

The man shook his head. "Just this one."

"Well, with all due respect, there are others in far worse shape." Kasey handed him a napkin. "Hold this against the wound and apply pressure. The paramedics will be here soon. They'll get you to the hospital and get the bullet out."

The man nodded and made his way over to the wall. Leaning against it, he sank to the floor and waited for the paramedics.

Next, Kasey found herself standing over a woman. One of the thieves stray shots had clipped her in her side.

"What's your name, dear?"

"Dear?" the woman asked incredulously. "I am Alanah Carrington, of the Southampton Carringtons. You will treat me with the respect I deserve."

Kasey took one look at the woman's stomach and handed her another serviette.

Pointing to the wound, Kasey muttered, "Well, Alanah, with an attitude like that, you can take care of yourself. I'd recommend you try to slow the blood flow. It doesn't look like the bullet has hit anything critical, but you will want to make sure you don't bleed out in the meantime."

She turned and walked off.

"Hey, come back here," the woman shouted after Kasey.

Kasey simply waved her off and moved on. She was not willing to waste time on condescending white privilege.

She made her way through the fallen guests. Some were already far beyond her ability to help. The submachine guns had reaped a heavy toll.

Others, Kasey patched up as best she could, offering encouragement and make shift medical attention of the non-magical variety.

Spotting Arthur Ainsley crouching over a man on the floor, Kasey made her way over to him. The man on the floor was middle-aged. His hair was parted neatly and swept to one side. He was dressed impeccably in a pinstripe suit, but Kasey couldn't help but note his suit seemed to be of a humbler vintage.

His white shirt was stained in red; he'd clearly been hit in the attack.

"Who is he, Arthur?" Kasey asked, as she crouched beside him.

"This is Cyrus Pillar and he is the head of the ADI. Or at least he was."

The ADI stood for the Anti Discovery Initiative. It was the law enforcement arm of the Arcane Council. Tasked with protecting the secrecy of the World of Magic, the ADI ensured witches and wizards registered with the council. They also sought to prevent the community from performing any reckless act of magic that would result in the discovery of their world.

Throughout history, discovery had always resulted in extreme hostility from the superstitious human population. Normals, or non-magical people as they were known, had always proved skeptical of those with special abilities. Only last week, Kasey had run into several of the ADI's agents when she'd inappropriately used her magic in the course of her investigation. After the ADI had cleaned up the mess, she'd been censured by the Council and warned against further infractions.

She looked at Cyrus. He'd been struck multiple times in the chest. Leaning over the body, she checked his pulse. In the mayhem, he'd already bled out.

"I'm so sorry, Chairman. He's gone."

As Kasey went to lift her hand away, a familiar mist descended over her eyes, bringing with it a vision.

CHAPTER SEVEN

*W*hen the mist cleared, Kasey was standing in the exhibition hall once more.

The gala's wealthy elite darted about in confusion as the armed thieves breached the hall. Kasey watched as the man known as the Khan raised his submachine gun into the air.

The submachine gun spat a burst of bullets into the ceiling.

Plaster rained from the roof as patrons fled from the armed intruders. They fled for the rear exits, only to find themselves face-to-face with more assailants who had cut off their retreat.

Kasey looked down and noted the familiar pinstripe suit. She knew at once that she was experiencing the night's events from Cyrus' point of view.

I don't know that this is entirely necessary. I need to focus my attention in the present, not flounder around in a past I have already witnessed.

Cyrus had been shot to death, that much was evident from the body. It didn't take any great deductive reasoning to work out how that had happened. Clearly, one of the thieves had caught him in the crossfire.

Kasey listened for the second time as Khan delivered his speech to the assembled patrons. He seemed awfully confident for a man robbing some of the richest people in the world.

How does he plan to escape? Kasey wondered to herself. Even if he were to successfully rob the gala and get out cleanly, he was still in the middle of New York City. The police would be all over them before they got more than a block from the museum.

Slowly but surely, the thieves corralled the gala's guests into the center of the room. With nowhere else to go, the patrons started ambling sideways toward the elaborate ice sculpture that ran along the wall of the exhibit.

Cyrus followed the other guests but began surveying the room, searching for an opening.

Kasey had never seen someone so calm under pressure. He scanned the clustered guests. Glancing down, Kasey caught a glimpse of his right hand. It had three fingers extended. As he began to raise his head, Kasey watched the fourth finger extend.

He's counting something, but what?

Cyrus smoothed his suit. Kasey felt something hard beneath the suit. From its position, she guessed there was a gun holster under his arm.

Clearly, the head of the ADI was looking for an opportunity to make his presence felt. Many of the security personnel in the room were doing the same. Unfortunately for them, they were outgunned, and they knew it.

While numbers were not in the thieves' favor, firepower was. If security drew their weapons, people would die, most of them innocent. The best they could hope for was for the robbery to end without bloodshed.

Kasey cringed as the exchange between Shakespeare and the aging patron unfolded yet again. Shakespeare's voice was firm, "The ring too, ma'am."

This time she knew exactly what was coming.

Mrs. Cardston firmly rebuffed the thief's demands. Once more, Stanley interceded. This time, Kasey could see his subtle footwork ensuring the thief could not see his left hand as it edged around to his holster.

Fortunately, when Stanley reached for his gun, Cyrus looked away. A movement to his left had drawn his attention. The thieves at the back door were huddled in conversation. Kasey was glad for the distraction. Some things didn't need to be seen twice.

One of the guests screamed as Stanley's gun bucked loudly.

The room erupted into chaos as guests ran in every direction.

Cyrus crouched. Staying low, he ran to the tables. As he flipped the nearest one on its end, plates and glasses fell to the floor and shattered. The upturned table provided some semblance of cover.

More gunshots echoed around the hall as the submachine guns roared to life. Bullets raced across the chamber, sending fountains of icicles blasting from the ornate sculpture as they struck home.

Cyrus turned and risked a look over the edge of the table. From his viewpoint, Kasey could see several of the thieves had already fallen, as had several of the patrons.

Crouching back down, Cyrus reached for his gun. A pair of legs halted directly in front of him, Cyrus stopped and looked up.

A waiter stood over him. The man was in his thirties, slim but fit. His skin was a deep olive complexion. He was of Mediterranean descent, clean-shaven but for a small goatee. In spite of the chaos, he was still clutching one of the silver serving trays with a lid.

To Kasey's surprise, the waiter threw off the lid and drew from the tray a pistol. He raised the weapon and pointed it directly at Cyrus.

Kasey tried to move but could not. She was trapped inside Cyrus body.

Without hesitation, the waiter drew a bead on Cyrus and fired.

Kasey felt the shooting pains in her chest as the bullets sank home. Fortunately, the mist descended, and the vision came to an end.

With the vision cleared, Kasey found herself in the exhibition hall still crouched over Cyrus's body. Her heart was pounding a million miles an hour. A chilled sweat ran down her face from the execution she had just witnessed.

This time she knew it was no accident.

Cyrus had been murdered.

Kasey stood up but almost passed out as her blood circulation returned to normal. Taking a moment to steady herself, she searched the room, looking for any sign of the waiter. In her mind's eye, she could see the young man with the olive complexion. He had been an unassuming bystander until he'd pulled his gun.

No one had caught the cold-blooded killing in the midst of the chaos. With bullets racing all around them, everyone else had been too concerned for their own safety. Kasey included. She felt a pang of guilt, despite knowing there was nothing she could have done for Cyrus.

She searched those still in the room. Among the patrons and wait-staff she could see, there was no one who fit her vision of the killer.

"What is it, Kasey?" Arthur asked. "What's wrong?"

"Yeah, Kasey, you look as white as a ghost," John added, sounding a little concerned. Her former tormentor-turned-date stood beside her.

Kasey didn't want to give away her gift. The Ainsleys may have known she was a witch, but her visions were her own and she planned to keep it that way. Nevertheless, their questions demanded answers, and she scrambled to find a suitable response.

"I don't know," Kasey replied. "In the chaos, I thought I saw someone else take a shot at Cyrus. I can't be sure, but I don't believe he was shot by the thieves. As strange as it sounds, I think one of the waiters killed him. If that's true, it means someone else in this room knew who he was and had an axe to grind with the ADI."

"Come now, Kasey. A waiter? That's absurd," Arthur said, raising his hand for silence.

"I know what I saw!" Kasey protested vehemently. "There was at least one other shooter here, maybe more."

"Perhaps he was an inside man," John suggested. "These sorts of robberies don't happen on their own."

"Perhaps," Kasey admitted.

Her vision had seemed far more like an execution than random happenstance, though. Likewise, there were no other bodies near Cyrus. If the waiter were truly working with the thieves, she would have expected there to be more bodies.

She was determined to find out where the waiter had disappeared to. He would have the answers she sought.

"John, can you look after those remaining here? I'm just going to duck out and check on those who are waiting outside. I want to make sure we don't have any other injuries.

John nodded. "Sure, go ahead. I've got things in here."

Kasey made her way across the exhibition hall. Shards of broken timber and glass were strewn across the room, results from the earlier gunfight. She took care to avoid the worst of it. For a moment, she regretted her lost heels. They lay somewhere in the debris.

She passed through the same door she had entered only a half-hour earlier. It seemed like an eternity ago now.

The exhibition was in ruin but there was no time for her to dwell on that now. She entered the hallway to find patrons everywhere.

Some were sitting, others standing. A few patrons lounged on benches scattered around the nearby sculpture exhibit. A steady stream of guests made their way toward the museum's rear entrance and the safety of Central Park.

Kasey was glad that at least a few of them were following instructions. She worried that the waiter may have already slipped out of the museum, though.

On her left, a group of waitstaff were congregating. At first glance, there were at least a dozen men and women in matching black pants and white shirts. Each of the men wore a black bow tie and cummerbund. The women wore black vests.

Under the guise of giving medical attention, Kasey approached them. "Are all of you okay?

Most of the staff nodded or gave affirmative responses.

One of them looked at Kasey and replied, "A few cuts and scrapes but nothing major here. Those still in the hall seem to have caught the worst of it. We're lucky to be alive."

One of the other men raised his hand in protest. "Lucky? If that idiot hadn't fired his weapon, maybe everyone would still be alive."

"Oh, shut up, Phil. We can't know that for sure. You're always so quick to blame everyone else."

"That's not true—" Phil began but Kasey cut him off.

"That's enough. We don't have time for this. The police will be here to take your statements soon. You can share your opinions then. In the meantime, we are trying to do a head count and see if anyone is missing."

Kasey surveyed the staff around her. None of them were a match for the man she had seen in her vision.

Frustrated, she pressed them for details. "Is this your full staff tonight?"

Phil replied, "We're still missing a few, two, maybe three."

"Any idea where they are?" Kasey asked.

"They might still be in the hall," the man replied. "They were nearest the entrance when the shooting started. I saw Tony go down. I don't know if he was hit or just avoiding the shooting. Janelle was with him. They haven't made it out yet."

Neither of them sounded like the man Kasey was hunting. He had been in the thick of things in the hall, hovering close to Cyrus waiting to strike.

"You said there were three missing?"

Phil shrugged. "There's Ben but I haven't seen him since the shooting started. Come to think about it, I haven't seen much of him at all tonight. It's possible he's slacking off somewhere. It wouldn't be the first time. There's a chance he wasn't even in the room when the attack happened."

Kasey seized at the possibility. "This Ben, what does he look like?"

Phil paused for a moment. "He's young, about your age. He looks like he's spent a lot of time in the sun, has a funny little goatee. It's a little pretentious."

Kasey clenched her fist in victory. Ben was the man she had seen in her vision.

"Has anyone seen him since the robbery?" she asked.

"Mmm," a woman to Kasey's left began.

"What?" Kasey turned toward the woman, her blonde hair was pulled back in a neat bun. "Have you seen him?"

The woman was shaking.

"I saw him head down the hall over there." She pointed down the dark corridor that ran from the central exhibition hall.

"I think he may have been looking for a bathroom or something. I haven't seen him since."

Without a second thought, Kasey took off down the hall.

At times, her visions were difficult to interpret, but the cold-blooded execution of Cyrus was impossible to misunderstand.

Ben had pulled the trigger, and Kasey wanted to know why.

Killing Cyrus in the middle of the robbery was a bizarre choice. There had been potential witnesses everywhere. Had it been a crime of opportunity, or something else?

There was no doubt Ben had chosen Cyrus deliberately. Of the hundreds of guests in the room, there were other targets with a far higher profile. Movie stars, billionaires, and politicians. Few would have any idea who Cyrus even was.

The waiter had wanted Cyrus dead, that much was clear. To make an attempt on the life of the head of the ADI in a room full of New York's elite made no sense whatsoever.

She ran down the corridor only to find herself in another large exhibition chamber filled with relics and treasures from Africa.

Dozens of priceless artifacts were on display. Kasey scanned the dark theater, looking for the missing waiter.

Out of the darkness, footsteps shuffled behind her.

She whirled around and came face-to-face with Ben.

Ben's eyes brows were narrowed in confusion. It was almost as if he had expected someone else. He recovered quickly.

Her heart raced as Ben adjusted the napkin resting over his right hand. Concealed beneath it was the same pistol Kasey had seen earlier. It was pointed at her chest.

Kasey was rooted to the spot. She felt as helpless as she had in her vision.

"Sorry, dear, you're just in the wrong place at the wrong time," he said.

Kasey's heart stopped altogether as she watched Ben pull the trigger.

CHAPTER EIGHT

*K*asey closed her eyes. The killer had caught her flat footed, and she didn't want to see what was coming.

It was surreal. The gunshot rang out as the breath was torn from her chest where the bullet slammed into her. The impact of the shot threw her off her feet.

Her ears were ringing from the gunshot. As the ringing faded, hurried footsteps fled down the darkened corridor, leaving her alone.

She couldn't breathe. Her chest was on fire. She lay there in the darkness waiting for the end to come, but it didn't.

After what seemed an eternity, her breath returned. Confused, Kasey raised her hand to her chest, searching for the wound.

She found nothing. She sat up and opened her eyes.

"Ow." She winced as the pain returned to her chest. Still, there was no sign of a gunshot. "There should be blood everywhere," she muttered as she checked her stomach and thighs.

There wasn't a drop of blood to be found anywhere.

She struggled to her feet. As she straightened to her full height, something fell on her foot. Bending down, she found a small lump of steel. It had rolled out the folds of her dress and landed on her toe. She picked it up, it was still warm.

"What the hell?" she muttered.

She realized it was the bullet from the waiter's gun. It had all the indicators of a bullet that had struck a solid surface.

As she wondered what had happened, Ernesto's voice came flooding back into her mind. "I picked that particular number not only because I thought you'd look fabulous in it, which you do, but I thought you might find it's other properties particularly useful given your track record."

"Ernesto, you sly dog, I could kiss you," Kasey said to the empty hall. The shimmering silver dress Ernesto had sold her was bullet-proof. Once again, Ernesto's foresight had saved her life. She smiled down at the dress. "Worth every penny."

Spinning around she searched for the waiter, but there was no sign of him. He was well and truly gone.

The sirens were closer now. From the sound of their piercing wail, they were just outside the museum. Had the Khan been apprehended trying to flee the scene?

Dusting herself off, Kasey hurried back to the European Sculpture exhibit to find it bustling with police and paramedics.

As expected, their response time had been blisteringly quick. Whether it was a call from within the museum, or the gunshots being overheard by the surging mass of paparazzi outside, someone had called 9-1-1.

Seeing things well in hand in the exhibit, Kasey made her way back to the central hall to check if she could help in anyway there.

Apart from the waiter's attempt to kill her, there hadn't been any other gunshots. The police would have locked the museum down and were now dealing with the aftermath of the bungled robbery.

It was madness, Kasey thought to herself. *To hit the museum during the biggest event of the year.* The attack was so brazen, it defied belief.

She entered the central exhibition hall. The earlier winter wonderland was no more. The room looked like a cyclone had struck it. Glass from a shattered chandelier littered the floor. The remnants of the broken fixture lay in a heap. Upturned tables lined the edge of the floor, the makeshift barricade that had saved countless lives.

The room was in disarray and a somber mood had settled over the hall like a storm cloud, displacing the room's earlier festive atmosphere.

Kasey tiptoed across the exhibition hall, trying to avoid the sea of broken glass. She'd only made it a few paces when a voice to her right called out to her.

"You alright, ma'am?"

Turning, Kasey found herself looking at the familiar face of Officer Henley. Officer Henley was a rookie at the Ninth Precinct, Kasey's station. She had only just finished working a case with him and his partner.

"Henley, good to see you,"

"Kasey, what are you doing here?" Henley interrupted. "Word around the station is that you were taking some time off. I heard you had a rough night last night." After glancing around the hall, he continued. "Tonight doesn't seem to have gone any better. Trouble seems to follow you around, Chase. Remind me never to invite you to my place."

Kasey smiled despite the circumstances. "Easy, Henley, this had nothing to do with me. I just happened to be in the wrong place at the wrong time.

"Story of your life, huh? Have you seen Bishop yet?"

Kasey shook her head. "No, I haven't. Is she here?"

"She sure is. Most of the precinct is for that matter. Even the chief."

"The chief? What's he doing here?"

"Mass shooting in the middle of New York City. Everyone is here, Kasey. In fact, half the cops in the city are here, or on their way. So are the paramedics, the fire department, and the bomb squad. Not to mention the press."

"Ah, the press." Kasey sighed.

"Someone must have tipped them off. They're flocking like vultures outside the cordon."

Kasey nodded. She should have expected that much. The gala was a disaster zone. With the number of celebrities present for the event, the morning news would feature little else.

"Where is the chief?" Kasey asked. "I need to speak to him."

"He's over there with the mayor." Henley pointed toward the door.

Chief West stood in the opening, locked in a hurried conversation with a squat, bespectacled man in his sixties.

The chief looked somber, but that was to be expected. This robbery-turned-tragedy would add to his already heavy workload. The attack would bring with it pressure from the families of the fallen victims. Being thrust in front of the world's press would add to the already considerable stress of his office.

"Henley, one more question," Kasey said. "Did you pick up anyone trying to leave the building?"

"Only some guests," Henley replied. "Why?"

"Two of the thieves fled on foot. I was hoping that they would have been picked up by the cordon."

Henley shook his head. "No such luck, Chase. It's chaos out there. We didn't even know that thieves made it out. I'll put the word out now, though. We'll see what we can do. Do you have any descriptions that we can work with? I'll put out an APB."

"Not much that will help. They are both dressed head to toe in black, with MP5's and a suicide vest. The leader was wearing a mask that made him look like Genghis Khan. I'm sure they will have ditched them by now, though."

"You're right, Chase. It's not much to go on. But I'll see what I can do."

"Thanks, Henley, I'm off to see the chief. If you see Bishop, tell her I'm looking for her."

"Will do," Henley replied as he headed down the hall to spread the word of the fleeing thieves.

Kasey approached the chief, unsure exactly what she wanted to say. She simply felt her account of the tragedy might be of value.

The chief looked up and locked eyes with her. His expression changed from somber to surprise.

"Miss Chase, when I authorized your personal leave, this isn't exactly how I expected you might use it."

"Hello, Chief. Trust me, this isn't what I had in mind when I came here tonight."

"Speaking of," the chief began, "how exactly did you come to be here? Not exactly the sort of crowd I'd have expected to see you in."

"I know, right?" Kasey replied. "My bank balance is a few zeros short of earning me an invite. I was here with the Ainsleys."

She was stretching the truth and she knew it. In light of how the evening's events had gone, she didn't feel the chief would respond well to her having broken into the gala.

"The Ainsleys?" the chief asked. "I wouldn't have expected you to be here with them either."

"You and me both," she replied. "But they reached out to me this morning, after we took down the serial killer. Arthur reached out to express his support. Personally, I didn't really feel like sifting through my grilled apartment, so a little bit of procrastination on my part and I ended up here."

Chief West nodded as he replied. "Last night, a serial killer. Tonight, this mess. If I were you, I'd lock myself in a little box and not go out tomorrow night."

"I'll take that advice on board, chief, but seriously, how much bad luck can one person have?"

"Let us both hope this is the end of it," he replied. "After this chaos, it will be all hands-on deck until we get this under control. Consider your leave revoked."

Kasey wanted to protest. She had planned on using her leave from the Department to investigate the organization that had sent Danilo to kill her.

"But Chief…"

"Kasey, it's done. We'll see you bright and early in the morning. Don't be late."

"Yes, chief," she said. There simply wasn't any other response he would accept. "So much for some rest."

"Don't be like that Kasey," he replied. "I'm sure we can find you a cell if you want it? No one will bother you there."

"I'll pass, thanks, chief. Maybe next time, though."

The chief was teasing but she knew better than to test him.

"Also, Chase, find Bishop. She will take your statement for tonight, and last night while you're at it. We need to wrap that up. Then go home and get some rest. It's safe to say we'll all be busy until this mess is put to rest. With a tragedy of this magnitude, the press will be all over us."

The press, Kasey's least favorite part of the job.

She changed the topic. "Speaking of Bishop, where I can find her?"

"Last I saw her, she was taking statements in the foyer out front. Head on out. I'm sure you'll find her there."

Kasey wasn't looking forward to seeing Bishop. She had dodged giving her statement at the precinct. In light of where she was and how she was dressed, not having time hardly seemed like a justifiable excuse. The reality was, the only other answers Kasey had to give, contained information that would reveal the existence of the world of magic.

Caught between the Council and her partner, Kasey had intentionally avoided giving a statement. Lying straight to Bishop's face made her uncomfortable and the last thing she needed was Bishop rooting around, searching for answers that Kasey couldn't give her.

With no way of avoiding Bishop, Kasey gave in and headed for the foyer.

The large entryway of the museum was as grand as the rest of the structure. Impressive art lined the walls, centuries of culture worth untold millions of dollars. Inside the foyer, a bevy of New York's wealthy elite gave statements to a group of police officers.

Beyond the large glass doors, the wall of press snapped away with their cameras, seeking to cover every aspect of the tragedy as it unfolded.

Kasey spotted Bishop through the crowd. She was taking a statement from one of the gala's guests. Kasey was surprised to see it was Mrs. Cardston, the woman whose refusal to surrender her ring had turned the robbery into a firefight. Against all odds, the woman had survived, no doubt in no small part due to Stanley's heroism.

Mrs. Cardston was a mess. Tears ran down her face as she struggled to give an account of the evening's events.

Kasey empathized with the woman as she knew what it felt like to be that close to death. Her experiences with Danilo had left her shaken to the core.

She waited patiently for Bishop to finish, standing just outside of Bishop's peripheral vision.

"Are there any other details you can give us that might help us track down the men who did this?" Bishop asked.

Mrs. Cardston dabbed at her eyes with a white handkerchief. "It all happened so fast. I just didn't see very much. I am sorry."

Bishop patted the woman on the back. "It's okay. That's normal during such a traumatic event. If you do remember anything else, here is my number." Bishop handed the woman her card and turned the page in her notepad, ready to take the next statement.

Here goes nothing. Kasey cut in front of the next guest, a man in a tux.

"Hey! I was next," the man called. "Some of us want to get out of here before midnight."

Kasey raised a hand to silence him. "I'll only be a minute, and she is my partner."

Bishop raised her head to Kasey. Her gaze travelled down Kasey as she took in the slinky silver dress. The color in her cheeks seem to grow redder and redder with every passing second.

"Look, Bishop..."

"Oh, I'm glad to see you made it to the party, Kasey," Bishop started. "You couldn't spare five minutes to give me a statement today but it's nice to know you could squeeze in a shopping trip and a gala."

"Bishop, it's not like that."

"It looks like that from here," Bishop replied. "As usual, you're running around getting into trouble and I'm here to clean up the mess. The least you could have done was take five minutes to tell me what happened last night."

The man in the tux pushed forward again. "Last night? Who cares what happened last night. There was a mass shooting here only minutes ago. Take this little spat and deal with it on your own time."

Kasey turned to the man and drove her finger into his chest. "Just like you, I've spent the last hour being shot at. Unlike you, however, I've spent the time since the attack trying to save as many lives as possible, while you've sat here waiting and complaining. My time is precious, there are people here who still need medical attention, and if you keep interrupting, you'll need it too."

"Did you just threaten me?" the man replied indignantly, his voice raising with each syllable.

"Oh, no, sir," Kasey responded, her voice dripping with sarcasm. "A threat is a verbose statement that men like you use to get their way. That, sir, was a promise. Now back off, before I decide to make good on it."

The man turned to Bishop for help.

Bishop simply shook her head. "I'd do what she says. Last night, she killed a man with her bare hands. It may have been self-defense, but she did it all the same. So, unless you want to take a chance with your life, I'd step back and give her the space."

The man in the tux grumbled as he stormed off.

"Look, Bishop," Kasey began. "I know you're upset but..."

"I'm not upset, Kasey. I'm angry," Bishop replied, cutting her off.

"About what?" Kasey asked shaking both her hands in exasperation. "I did exactly what you asked. It's not like I ran off and got myself in trouble, or intentionally tried to tackle the killer without you. I stayed in the station just like you asked. Unfortunately, so did he. He knocked me out and kidnapped me from the morgue. It was hardly my choice."

"You think I don't know that?" Bishop shook her head as she avoided meeting Kasey's gaze. "I'm not angry at you, Kasey. I'm angry at myself. I'm angry that I didn't see through his stupid little ruse. I'm angry that I didn't even run his credentials through our system, and most of all, I'm angry that I left you alone when you needed me most."

Kasey realized her mistake. She'd believed herself to be the target of Bishop's anger. Now she knew better. It wasn't directed at her at all. She'd just been collateral damage.

"Don't beat yourself up, Bishop," Kasey replied putting her arm around Bishop. "You've done far more for me in the last ten days than anyone else for a long time. You have put your life and your career on the line for me and I'm grateful for it."

"That's not the worst of it," Bishop replied as she tapped her notepad against her palm. "I'm mostly upset about why I did let him slip past my guard. I should have known better than to trust him, but

I let his husky voice get under my guard. I should have known better, I guess I'm just..."

"Just what?" Kasey asked softly.

"Just frustrated," Bishop answered, looking down at her feet. "I guess I just thought my life would be further along by now. I am thirty-five and I'm still single. I haven't had a serious relationship in almost five years and I guess I'm a little worried that life is passing me by."

Kasey was gob smacked. She'd never seen this side of Bishop. She was withdrawn and vulnerable. It was unlike the Diane Bishop she had come to know in her brief time at the NYPD.

"Look, Bishop." Kasey drew Bishop in for a hug. "You're the strongest woman I've ever met. You may be thirty-five but you're already a detective in the NYPD. What's more, you're killing it in a city where crime never sleeps. You have one of the highest closure rates of anyone in the precinct. Maybe the city.

"Don't beat yourself up because you're down a boyfriend. Any man would be lucky to have you. I think that they, like everyone else in the city, might be just a little intimidated by you. Hang in there. You'll find a man with the balls to ask you out, or maybe you'll have to ask him. Either way, it'll be worth the wait. You don't need a man to define you. You kick ass all on your own."

Bishop raised her head. "Thanks, Kasey. I really needed that."

She wiped her eye to prevent a tear from rolling down her cheek.

"Hey, Bishop. I know now probably isn't a good time, but the chief wanted me to give you my statement both for last night and tonight."

"Now is as good a time as any," Bishop replied.

"Where do you want to start?" Kasey asked. "Tonight, or last night?"

"Oh, I think I have a pretty good idea what happened last night," Bishop replied. "I saw the scene after all, and you just filled in most of the blanks. Tell me about tonight. I want to know what happened and more importantly, I want to know how the heck you managed to get an invite to the gala?"

Kasey considered her words carefully. "Any chance we can talk off the record, just for a moment?"

Bishops eyes narrowed, as they bored into Kasey's soul. "You didn't get an invite to the gala, did you Kasey?"

"Perhaps not in the regular sense of the word."

"So, you broke in?" Bishop asked.

"I would call it gatecrashing at worst," Kasey replied. "How does that rank on a scale of misdemeanor through to felony?"

Bishop sighed. "Gatecrashing Kasey? The courts call it break and entering and you could get seven years for it."

CHAPTER NINE

*M*orning found Kasey back at the station and on active duty as the chief had dictated. Her holiday of a single day was over, and she was back at the grindstone. The tragedy at the gala had dominated the evening news. With suspects still at large, the tension in the precinct was palpable.

Kasey was working on her reports when a cheery voice cut through the silence of the morgue. "Well, I heard someone was the belle of the ball."

"Morning, Vida," Kasey said as he stepped into the room.

As always, he was cheerier than Kasey thought possible at such an early hour.

"And a good morning to you. I have to say, Kasey, things have certainly spiced up since you arrived. I remember a time when we actually had days between killings in this city. I even had the time to investigate a few accidental deaths here and there. Now it's all serial killings and mass shootings. Definitely a change of pace, that's for sure."

"Don't blame me, Vida." Kasey replied putting down her pen. "These lunatics were here before me, and I imagine they'll be here long after I'm gone. It's just unfortunate that they all seem to have come out of the woodwork in the last few weeks."

"Perhaps," Vida mused raising a finger. "Though you must admit, the bizarre seems to follow you like your own personal storm cloud. At least while your tenure here lasts, we know there'll never be a dull moment. Speaking of the bizarre, that killer's body, the one from your apartment, it never did get located. You're sure it wasn't here yesterday when you came in?"

"Definitely not," Kasey replied shaking her head. "I would remember seeing the body of the man who tried to kill me, don't you think?"

There was no way she could tell him what had truly happened. She simply hoped that if she deflected him for long enough, he would put the lost body down to bureaucratic inefficiency and move on.

She couldn't have him digging around looking for answers. The Arcane Council would not put up with it, and Kasey didn't quite trust them to deal with Vida kindly. They had warned as much when he'd unknowingly submitted a strand of Werewolf hair to the FBI for analysis.

Vida may have been inquisitive but as far as bosses go, he was one of the best she'd ever had. She didn't want to have to gamble on a replacement and she'd grown rather fond of the English-born Indian, and his quirky sense of humor.

"That's odd," Vida said drumming his fingers on the steel table, "because the uniforms that brought him in assured me that they left him here on the examination table."

"I don't know what to tell you, Vida. Have you checked the drawers?"

"Twice," Vida replied holding up two fingers for emphasis. "Not a sign of him anywhere."

Kasey shrugged and through up her hands. "Sorry, I wish I could help but I have no idea."

Vida shrugged. "Oh, well, I'm sure it will turn up eventually. In the meantime, we'll need to get to work on the bodies from last night. With the publicity in the press, there is a ton of pressure on West. You can guess what that means for us."

"Yeah, the chief isn't much for the media. I suppose it's full steam ahead to process the bodies. At least that way we can get their families some closure," Kasey replied.

"There is that," Vida answered. "We also need to find out anything from them. We still need a lead on the two that got away."

"So, still no word?" Kasey asked shuffling her papers back into their folder to clear space. "I figured we'd have nabbed them by now. How far could the two of them have gotten on foot?"

"Farther than we thought, evidently. They must've slipped out of the museum undetected before the perimeter was established. Patrols have been scouring the city all night, but still no sign of them."

"Clearly they had thought through the possibility of the alarm being raised. They hit the gala knowing they could make it out in time. The only thing they don't seem to have planned on was just how attached a few rich folks would be to their trinkets. Clearly, they were smarter than we gave them credit for."

"I don't know about that," Vida replied. "Six of them are dead. One of them in is in the hospital in critical condition and the other is in custody downstairs.

"The two of them that did get away, did so empty-handed. Now they have nothing to show for their efforts and a rap sheet that will land them life in prison if they are caught.

"Now every cop in New York City is after them. Last night's shooting left twenty-two people dead. Several more are in critical condition. When they are caught, they'll be lucky if they're not charged with terrorism as well. A jury of their peers will make sure they spend the rest of their life behind bars."

"The part I don't get is the vests," Kasey replied. "I saw the explosive. But despite the firefight, not a single one went off. Talk about lucky."

"That's the interesting part, Kasey," Vida answered. "The vests were fake. The bomb squad took them apart last night. Nothing but painted clay and a few wires to look the part. They were hoping the threat would be enough to deter anyone from taking a shot at them. It's a hell of a bluff when you think about it. Shame it didn't pay off for them. The whole thing might have ended without a shot fired."

Just one more bizarre detail in a very strange night.

"What was it like?" Vida asked. "I've always wondered what I would do if I was stuck in a situation like that."

"It was chaos," Kasey admitted. "Everything happened so fast. At first, we were just trying to survive. There were so many of them. It's a miracle more people weren't killed."

"There is a dozen more in the hospital, Kasey, I'm sure they would disagree with you."

"You weren't there, Vida. It was a shooting gallery and we were lined up like sitting ducks. There should have been far more casualties."

Then Kasey realized it.

The words of Arthur Ainsley came flooding back into her mind. Many of the Arcane Council had been there, along with their security. The council must have subtly used their powers to shield as many people as they could. Without them, the death toll could have been enormous.

In the thick of the shooting, Kasey hadn't even noticed them at work. She knew that John's spell had saved her life. The subtle little incantation had jammed one of the thief's weapons as he had drawn a bead on Kasey. Doubtless the other witches and wizards had been at work mitigating as much of the carnage as they could.

"So, where do you want to start?" Vida's question drew Kasey from her reflection.

"Start on what?" Kasey asked.

"Examining the bodies," Vida replied. "You know that thing we do here... work... as medical examiners... I'm a little worried that I have to spell this out for you. Are you sure you're all right?"

"Yes, of course," Kasey said. "Sorry, I was just deep in thought. It's been a crazy few days."

"Let's get to it," Vida said pointing to the wall of refrigerated drawers lining the morgue's wall. " You're up first, Kasey. Pick a number between one and twenty-two."

"It's going to be a long day, isn't it?" Kasey asked as she hung up her jacket and pulled on her fluid-resistant jumpsuit.

"You bet," Vida answered, reaching for his own.

"Then I guess number one," Kasey replied.

"How boring," Vida answered. "I'd have gone with number seventeen."

"Then perhaps you shouldn't have asked," Kasey said. "You know what they say about starting at the very beginning."

"Yes," Vida replied, unimpressed. "It is a very good place to start. It is also the worst musical of all time."

"Darn, you have seen it. I was hoping to stump you with that one."

"Never," Vida answered. "I had a childhood too, once. Fortunately, now I have far more choice in the movies I watch."

"I'm sure you loved it," Kasey insisted, doing her best impression of Julie Andrews. "Do re mi..."

Vida shook his finger at Kasey. "I will sack you if you so much as finish that sentence." His smile robbed the threat of any malice. "Now get over here and help me with the body."

Kasey followed Vida over to the steel drawers that lined the wall. The refrigeration unit allowed the morgue to preserve the bodies of the fallen until they had the opportunity to examine them properly. Rarely were so many needed at a single time, but the evening's tragedy had them filled to capacity.

Vida opened the top, leftmost draw, and pulled it out Kasey pushed a gurney over until it rested beside the drawer.

"You're going to need to put your back into it, Kasey, help me get him down. This is one heavy nob."

She reached up and together, she and Vida struggled under the weight of the body as they lifted it on to the gurney.

Vida took a deep breath. "Honestly, Kasey, of all the bodies, you had to pick the most out of shape of the lot of them."

"Well, best we got him down now while it's early and we're still fresh." Kasey replied. "There is no way I'd be lugging him around at four thirty. Who is he, anyway?"

Vida wheeled the gurney into the center of the room and together they heaved the body onto the autopsy station. Picking a file off the table, Vida introduced the victim.

"This, Kasey, is the body of one Reginald Mornington. Until his untimely death last night, Mr. Mornington was the third richest man in the continental United States. He spent his life in the coal mining game and was well known both for his poor luck at the gambling table and for his love of fine cuisine."

Kasey examined the man. Heavily overweight and in his sixties, it seemed a miracle that he had not suffered a heart attack years earlier.

"Well, unfortunately for Mr. Mornington, his luck hasn't changed. Bullets don't really care what your net worth is," Kasey answered

Vida nodded as he counted the man's wounds. "Indeed they do not, Kasey. Mr. Mornington, he managed to find three of them. Not at all surprising, really. I imagine he was an easy target."

"Come on Vida, that's just cruel," Kasey replied.

"Cruel, but true," Vida replied, holding up a finger. "It appears he took two in the stomach, before the third bullet struck him near his heart. We won't know until we open him up, but I suspect it will have nicked his left coronary artery, resulting in his death."

"Well, Vida, where would you like to begin?"

"As the cause of death is readily apparent, we will focus our energy and efforts on gathering evidence that will help us bring these men to justice. We can perform a more complete autopsy later if need be, but for the time being, let us remove the bullets so that Forensics can run ballistics tests on them.

"We have three entry points and no exit wounds, so it is safe to say all three of them are still lodged inside Mr. Mornington. It's time to get them out. Scalpel, please."

"I'm not your nurse," Kasey answered. "Get it yourself."

"Very well," Vida replied, fetching a scalpel off the tray. "I'll start on the one near his heart. You can take the two in his belly."

Kasey lifted a second scalpel and set to work.

She had always had a strong stomach, and the wonders of the human body never ceased to amaze her. In spite of its frail appearance, the human body was surprisingly resilient. Unfortunately, even resilience has a limit, and three nine-millimeter rounds usually found that limit pretty quickly.

Kasey made an incision over the wound to allow for easier retrieval of the bullet. She drew a set of medical forceps off the table and set to work, searching for the first bullet.

Her hands worked on autopilot while she went over the case in her mind. It just didn't make sense to hit the gala, even with a getaway plan and the dummy explosives to deter a response. It was still a risky move. Such a high-profile event was certain to have private security by the boatload.

There are less heavily defended banks in New York, Kasey thought as she found the first bullet. Working the forceps, she drew it out and dropped the bullet into a steel pan. The round clanged around the base of the tray before coming to rest.

"Come on, slow poke," she said as Vida continued searching for the bullet lodged near Mornington's heart.

Vida didn't look up from his work. "There's still one more down there. Grab that one too while you're at it."

"As you wish," Kasey replied, returning to work.

Her mind wandered to the waiter. Cyrus had not been a random target. What she had witnessed in her vision was an execution. Whoever this Ben was, he had a grudge to bear out with Cyrus, or possibly the ADI. Of the twenty-two victims, Cyrus stood apart.

He was the only one who had been killed with any degree of fore-thought.

How had the Arcane Council wronged you, Ben?

She replayed the incident in her mind. Her vision was not ambiguous at all. Cyrus' death had been cool, calculated murder. If the robbery had been allowed to run its course, the thieves would have escaped, and the gala would have been investigated as a robbery rather than a massacre.

Had that happened the waiter would have still been there seeking for an opportunity to kill Cyrus. While the two crimes had taken place together, Kasey could see they were independent of one another.

Anyone who has a problem with the ADI and Cyrus could also prove a danger to other members of the magical community.

I have to find out who he is and where he is now.

It would be difficult to divert resources away from the manhunt for the missing thieves, but Kasey knew the waiter was important. The man hadn't thought twice about taking a shot at her. If it hadn't been for her dress and Ernesto's foresight, she would also be dead.

Thinking about the encounter, Kasey began to wonder why the waiter had loitered in the museum. Surely after killing Cyrus it would have been in his best interest to stash his weapon and flee the museum in the ensuing chaos.

What had he been waiting for?

Clang.

The sound of another bullet striking the steel pan drew Kasey from her thoughts.

"Oh, come now, Kasey, with that much padding, the bullet couldn't have made it very far. Mine was buried beside his heart and I still managed to get it out. Chop, chop, we need to keep this moving."

Kasey focused on her task. Within minutes, she located her bullet and drew it out before setting it in the pan.

"Well that's two Vida, to your one. By any account, I'm winning."

"I wasn't aware we were racing," Vida replied. "Don't burn all your energy now, there are still twenty-one to go. This is a marathon, not a sprint."

"You really think you'll do any better at a marathon, Vida? I think I clock more hours in the gym than you even think about exercise. You don't stand a chance."

"We'll see about that, Kasey. Bag those bullets, we'll see what our friends in forensics can come up with."

Kasey pulled out an evidence bag and proceeded to pour the three bullets into it. Then, she labeled the bag and set it aside. "There we go."

"Very well, Mr. Mornington. Let's get you back into cooler climates while we take a look at Mrs. Mornington. More precisely, the third Mrs. Mornington."

"The third?" Kasey asked

"Yes, apparently Mr. Mornington was far more adept at finding wives than keeping them. According to his records, he was married to Mrs. Mornington eighteen months ago in a lovely ceremony on Long Island."

Kasey and Vida struggled to get Mr. Mornington back into the drawer. When the latch finally clicked shut, Vida opened the second drawer and drew out Mrs. Mornington. Kasey found herself looking down at a woman who couldn't have been much older than she was. The slender blonde was well toned, a stark contrast to her husband.

"As you can see Kasey, they married for love," Vida taunted.

"Very funny," Kasey replied.

"What's funny?" a voice called from the door.

Looking over her shoulder, Kasey spotted Bishop standing in the doorway of the morgue.

"Hey, Bishop, what brings you down to our neck of the woods?" Vida asked as he retrieved the gurney.

"I wanted to see what progress you are making here," Bishop replied strolling into the morgue. "Find me anything I can use?"

"I hate to disappoint you, Bishop, but we've only just started and it's early days yet. We have hours of work ahead of us just to process these bodies, "Vida answered. "Forensics hasn't even started on the bullets yet. I doubt we'll have anything for you before this afternoon."

"Not to worry, Vida. I'm sure you'll get through it. Unfortunately, I am going to have to deprive you of your assistant. I need Kasey's help upstairs."

Kasey sighed in relief. The thought of even a temporary reprieve from the pile of work ahead of her was a welcome interruption.

"Upstairs? What for?" Vida demanded.

"We're going to interrogate a prisoner and I need Kasey's help. After all, she was there. By all accounts, she was the one that choked him out. Without her, we would have nothing."

"You choked him out?" Vida asked, his mouth agape. "Thieves armed with submachine guns, and your idea was to strangle one of them into submission?"

Kasey held up her hands to cut them off. "That's not the whole story, Bishop, and you know it. Besides, the security detail dropped one of the other thieves, as well, so we would still have someone to question."

Bishop's face fell a little.

"What, Bishop? What's wrong? What aren't you telling me?"

"The other thief died in hospital this morning, Kasey. The trauma from his wounds was too severe. The doctor went to check on him and found that he had died in his sleep. Now the thief left in holding is all we have. We need to shake him and see what we can get out of him."

Kasey nodded. She had seen the wounded thief go down, but she'd passed him by, when tending to the wounded. She had focused her efforts on the innocent victims, rather than those who had brought misery to the gala in the first place.

Based on what she had witnessed in the shootout, she had figured his wounds were superficial. His death came as a complete surprise.

"Well, what are you waiting for, Kasey? Are you in or out?" Bishop gesturing to the door.

"In, of course," Kasey replied, tearing off her jumpsuit. "What's the plan?"

Bishop was all business. The vulnerable partner Kasey had seen the night before was gone. In measured tones, she replied, "He's facing twenty-two consecutive life sentences. We are going to scare the hell out of him, and then we're going to shake him until he gives us something we can use."

CHAPTER TEN

The interrogation room was a small, square chamber. Its concrete walls were purposely painted a lifeless grey, designed to imitate a jail cell it sent a clear message. Those who found themselves here were simply a step away from charges that would see them behind bars. The only noteworthy features were a large one-way mirror allowing interrogations to be observed. The second was the security camera situated over the door to keep a record of proceedings.

Opposite them sat their prisoner. Deprived of his Elvis mask he presented a different image. His dark beady eyes studied Kasey as she in turn examined him. Slight swelling indicated his nose may have been broken recently.

Detective Bishop gently placed a manila folder on the table. "Tyson Kovacs, I am Detective Bishop. I trust you have had a pleasant evening. I don't imagine this is how you expected it would end."

"I want my lawyer," Kovacs replied. "I have rights, you know. I want my phone call, and I want my lawyer here now."

Bishop leaned forward. "Afraid to disappoint you, Mr. Kovacs, but both your phone call and your lawyer will have to wait. We have some important questions for you and time is of the essence."

"You can't question me without a lawyer present. I understand my rights, you know."

"Of course you do, Mr. Kovacs. This isn't your first time in the system, is it? In fact, you have more than a dozen misdemeanors on your record. Granted, nothing as grandiose as last night but certainly nothing to be ashamed of.

"Mr. Kovacs, in the past, your crimes have been at the petty end of the spectrum. Unfortunately for you, when you strode into the museum armed with automatic weapons and explosive vests, your rap sheet became all the more impressive. You're not being held for armed robbery or even murder, Mr. Kovacs. You're being held as a terror suspect."

"A terrorist? Are you kidding me?" Kovacs shouted, his handcuffs jangling as he slammed his fist into the table.

Kasey jumped, but Bishop simply leaned back in her chair.

"I'm not kidding at all, Mr. Kovacs. What you may or may not be aware of, are the differences in the rules governing the treatment of suspected terrorists as opposed to ordinary thieves.

"Even though they might be US citizens like yourself, your rights are not what they once were. Don't worry, this isn't Hollywood. We can't torture you, but the Miranda rights that you've clearly become accustomed to relying on, won't serve you here now as they have in the past.

"What a load of..."

"I assure you, Mr. Kovacs," Bishop replied, cutting him off, "that here in New York, we are well-acquainted with our rights and processes when dealing with those suspected of committing terrorist actions on United States soil.

"Moreover, I will inform you that your Miranda rights are able to be waived in the instance that we believe the lives of other citizens may yet be in danger, a position that is more than plausible given the escape of two of your party last night.

"The man known as the Khan and one other of your compatriots managed to escape undetected. While they remain at large, we have every reason to believe that further terrorist incidents may occur and therefore, your Miranda rights are to be waived until such a time as we can ascertain they are no longer a threat."

"We're thieves, not terrorists," Kovacs replied. "It was a robbery gone wrong. The vests were just to ensure that the private security behaved themselves. you know the type. Those sorts of gun-toting maniacs are always trigger-happy. The threat of a bomb was meant to keep them in check."

"Shame that wasn't the case last night," Bishop replied. "If it were, you might only be here dealing with an armed robbery charge rather than twenty-two counts of first degree murder. Not to mention any other charges that may yet be filed."

"Twenty-two? I didn't shoot anyone."

"Well, we both know that isn't true," Kasey said tapping the table, "After all, I was there."

Kovacs took a closer look at Kasey. "You're the little wretch that choked me out."

"That is correct, sir," Kasey replied, motioning with her hand as if she were adding points to a chalk board. "I had a perfect view of you as you fired your weapon into the crowd of guests. When my colleague and I are finished pulling the bullets out of the victims downstairs, I'm sure we'll find more than enough that match your weapon. After all, with ten thieves and twenty-two victims, the odds are that at least two of them are yours. Maybe more. I guess we'll soon see."

"Yes, and then for any you didn't kill directly, you'll be treated as an accessory," Bishop added. "So, don't worry, Tyson, this room is likely the biggest one you will see for the rest of your life. Apart from a small stint in a courtroom, of course. But Tyson, if you think a jury of your peers is going to save you, you are dumber than you look, and that's saying something."

Tyson Kovacs sat back in his chair. "Well, obviously you want something. What is it? Make me your best offer."

"Our best offer?" Bishop answered. "Why, you have been here before, haven't you? Unfortunately, for you, Mr. Kovacs, there is only one offer and it's this.

"We have you and one of your colleagues in custody. Granted he is in a little worse condition than you. It seems he got shot up a little in the fight but nothing terminal. The doctors assure me is out of surgery and will be waking up shortly.

"When he does, we'll go and talk with him and get the information we are looking for. So, my offer is this: either you spill the identity and location of the man known as the Khan, or we can get it from your friend. It doesn't really matter to us which one gives us the information, but rest assured, one of you will give it to us.

"The other will be thrown at the courts. Your choice, Kovacs."

Kasey did her best to hide her surprise. She recognized the brilliance in Bishop's plan. Kovacs had been in custody all night; there was no way he would know the other thief was already dead.

Time was a powerful motivator. The notion that at any moment his comrade might wake up and talk, to save his own skin, was weighing on Kovacs. Kasey could see the defeat in his eyes as he considered his options.

While Kovacs may have been willing to keep a secret on his own, knowing that there was someone else out there ready to rat him out and leave him carrying the bag for the crime was eating away at him.

"Whoever you've got, he won't talk either. We all know better than to cross the Khan," Kovacs answered, folding his arms.

Bishop nodded. "Okay, Kovacs. Well, we can leave you here to have a bit of a think about it. We're going to go and wait for a call from the hospital.

"Just remember, your deal expires the second he talks. Whoever gives us the Khan gets the deal. We'll put in a word for them with the district attorney, ensure they face a lesser charge. Whichever of you stays silent, well, we'll throw you under the bus.

"Your choice, Kovacs. You sit here and have a bit of a think about just how confident you are that he'll stay silent. After all, you're safe in police custody but your friend, he's in the hospital. Unfortunately for him, he got shot in the leg, so he won't be running away from anyone. If the Khan is wanting to cover his tracks, and I'm betting he will, your friend is in mortal danger.

"Personally, I think he's far more likely to see things our way. Don't take my word for it, though. Sit there. Have a think about it. Let me know what you come up with."

Bishop slid back, her chair grinding against the concrete floor as she stood up. Pointing to the clock on the wall, she stated, "The clock's ticking, Kovacs. See that you don't let it run out of time."

Kasey followed Bishop back into the bullpen. Closing the door behind them, they left Kovacs alone with his thoughts.

"Well, I imagine that has given him something to think about," Bishop said with a smile.

"That was pretty clever, Bishop," Kasey nodded approvingly. "There aren't many detectives that could pull off a prisoner's dilemma with only one suspect."

"Thanks, Kasey. I figured he wouldn't know any better. He may yet call our bluff, but I doubt it. Last night will see him spending the rest of his life in a super max. I don't think he has it in him. He just needs a bit of a push."

"Well, you certainly gave him that," Kasey replied, patting Bishop on the back. "I take it you're feeling a little better?"

Bishop nodded. "A little. The last few days have been rough, but I'll get through. It's nice to know you have me covered."

"What are partners for?" Kasey replied.

"Well, until last night, I figured your purpose in life was to get in trouble and drag me into the line of fire," Bishop replied with a grin.

"Ow," Kasey said as she mimed pulling a knife out of her back. "I believe this is yours." She handed the imaginary knife to Bishop.

"Just kidding, Kasey. Thanks for your help last night. I really needed it. From here on, it's upward and onward. We have to find these lunatics. If they are bold enough to try something like the gala, they are far too dangerous to be left on the street. We need to pick them up before they cause any more trouble."

"It's true," Kasey answered. "They are dangerous."

"What are you thinking, Kasey? I feel a *but* coming on."

Kasey laughed. "Not so much of a *but* as an <u>also</u>. Last night, when we talked about the shooting, I left out one detail."

Bishop sighed. "Really? I thought we were past this."

"We are, Bishop," Kasey insisted. "But last night there was far too much going on. I knew if I mentioned anything you would all think I was nuts."

"Think?" Bishop replied with a tight smile. "Kasey, I know you're crazy. I know you broke into a house on your own while stalking a serial killer. I've always had my doubts about your sanity, so go ahead and spell it out. I doubt it'll change anything."

Kasey took the good-natured taunt in stride. "Well, last night when the shooting started, there was chaos. Bullets flying everywhere, people screaming, it was madness. Everything went to hell, but I swear, I saw a waiter pull a gun and kill one of the guests."

Bishop sucked her bottom lip into her mouth and said nothing.

"I know what you're thinking, Bishop."

"You're right, Kasey, that does sound crazy. Even if there was an inside man, why would he give himself away when the robbery went sideways?"

"See, that's what I've been struggling with. I don't think he was one of the thieves. I saw him shoot a man twice in the chest at almost point-blank range. In the chaos, I don't know that anyone else even noticed it, but I saw it clear as day. It was an execution."

"You can see how this sounds, right?"

"Yes, I can. That's why I said nothing last night. The victim was on the other side of the table to the thieves. When we found his body, he was sitting against the upturned table with his back to the other shooters. If they had shot him through the table, his wounds would have been in his back not his chest. He was shot by someone on our side of the hall and I saw the man who did it."

Bishop leaned against the desk. "You realize he could've been shot by the thieves and then collapsed against the table, right?"

"You're right, he could have, but that's not what I saw. Check the security cameras, you'll see it too," Kasey clenched her fists in frustration. "The waiter drew a gun, shoot him twice in the chest at point-blank range, and then disappear into the chaos. I went looking for him after the shooting stopped and couldn't find him anywhere. But I'm not crazy, Bishop. I spoke to the other staff and he exists. His name is Ben."

Bishop Shook her head. "Unfortunately, the cameras were sabotaged. Nothing inside the hall was being recorded."

Kasey let out a deep breath. "Of course they were."

Before Bishop could reply, a voice called out from across the bullpen.

"Bishop, the suspect is asking for you. It sounds like he's ready to talk," Johnson called.

Bishop leaned toward Kasey. "I'm not saying I don't believe you, but we have to deal with the Khan first. If we don't catch the Khan, heads will roll.

"So, let's start with Kovacs. We'll find out who the Khan is behind that mask and where we can find him. Once we have the Khan in custody, we will go after this waiter of yours. Okay?"

"Sure." Kasey nodded reluctantly. "Sounds like a plan."

She followed Bishop back to the interrogation room.

As the door swung open, Bishop gloated. "You know, Kovacs, that was even quicker than I expected. I'm almost disappointed."

"You won't be when I'm through telling you what I know," Kovacs replied, "but before I do, we're talking deal."

"Oh, yeah, and what did you have in mind?" Bishop asked.

"I'm a thief, not a killer," Kovacs said. "I got recruited for the gala job. Payment was fifty grand upfront and a share of the take when we were done. It was meant to be a quick job, in and out. No one was meant to get hurt. We were told the one percent wouldn't miss their jewelry."

Bishop sat down and popped her recorder on the middle of the table. "Mind if I put this on the record?"

Kovacs shook his head. "As I said, I didn't think anyone was going to get injured. The guns and vests were just meant to dissuade the private security. They aren't mall cops. No offense."

Bishop glared at Kovacs. "None taken. Now tell us something we don't know. Who is the Khan?"

"First, we talk deal," Kovacs said. "Without it, there is no way I'm gonna give you a damn thing."

"Fine," Bishop replied. "Spit it out and I'll see what I can do. It is going to be hard to weasel out of the mass murder charge. The District Attorney is going to have to be persuaded. He'll need a smoking gun. *The* smoking gun."

"It shouldn't be that hard to convince him," Kovacs said. "I'm sure you'll finish analyzing the scene soon enough. Like I said, I'm a thief, not a murderer. When your techs run ballistics, they will find that I didn't kill a single person."

"I saw you fire your weapon," Kasey countered. "I saw it with my own eyes."

"That's right." Kovacs looked at her. "Before the job, I switched out my rounds for blanks. If things went wrong, I didn't want to go down for murder. You check those bodies. You'll find I didn't kill a single person. Like I said, I'm a thief not a killer."

"Well, we'll see about that," Bishop countered as she leaned across the table. "If you did in fact not kill anyone, there is every chance that we can have your sentence reduced, possibly even commuted, but that will be based entirely on the strength of the information you give us. So, think carefully."

Silence descended on the interrogation room. Bishop began drumming her fingers on the table.

"No jail time. That's the deal," Kovacs said. "If I snitch on the others, I'm a dead man. There isn't a prison in this country where I'll be safe. If I give you a name, I need witness protection. That's the deal. Anything else, and I may as well say nothing at all. I'll take my chance in the courts. You get me that deal and I give you a name. Nothing else will do."

"Fine!" Bishop answered, slamming her palm against the table. "Time is of the essence, Kovacs. We need a name and we need it now."

"Then I guess you better make a call, detective," Kovacs countered. "Because I'm not opening my mouth again until I know you have the authority to make that deal."

"I get it," Bishop said. "Give me a moment."

She pulled out her phone and dialed it. There was a nervous pause as the phone began to ring.

After what seemed like an eternity the phone was picked up. "Oh, hello Bruce, it's Detective Bishop from the Ninth Precinct. Can I speak with District Attorney Ryder please? Yes, I'll hold"

Bishop tapped her foot as she held the phone to her ear, grim expression in place. Whoever the Khan was, clearly Kovacs was afraid of him. He would rather go to prison than risk being identified as the snitch who had given up the Khan.

"Ah, Lawrence, it's me, Diane," Bishop said into the phone.

Kasey's eyebrow crept up. No one called Bishop by her first name.

"Sorry to bother you at work, Lawrence, but I need a favor. We have one of the perps here from last night's shooting. Long story short, he insists he didn't kill anyone. He has information that could help us catch the ringleader and the other thief who are still in the wind. Unfortunately, the only way he's talking is if we drop charges and put him in witness protection. It seems he'd rather risk jail than give up whoever was behind the robbery without protection. Any chance that you'll work with us on that basis?" Bishop nodded against her phone. "Thanks Lance, I owe you one."

She hung up the phone and looked at Kovacs.

"Well, you have your deal. It's contingent on two things, though. One, that you didn't kill anyone. If evidence from the scene contradicts your testimony here, it will impact your deal. Second, you must give us something substantial that will not only identify the Khan but bring him to justice."

Kovacs smiled. "No worries on that count, detective. As for part one of our deal, I have no doubt the evidence will exonerate me. As for part two, I can give you the name but if you want to bring him to justice, you are going to have to move fast, because once he cleans house, I imagine he'll skip town. If he goes underground, you won't see him again for years."

"A name, Kovacs. That's the deal," Bishop nudged.

Kovacs paused for a moment, then said, "His name, detective, is… Wendell Samson."

CHAPTER ELEVEN

*B*ishop's jaw dropped. "Wendell Samson. a.k.a. the Ghost. That Wendell Samson?"

Kasey was at a loss. She'd never heard of this Wendell Samson. Pulling out her phone Kasey took to the internet for answers.

Kovacs nodded. "One and the same. Why do you think I wasn't talking without a deal? There isn't a man alive who would cross Samson and expect to live. That's why I want witness protection. In prison, I'm as good as dead. At least in witness protection I'll have a fighting chance."

"You give us the information we need to take him down," Bishop began "and we'll make sure you have more than a fighting chance." She stood and leaned over the table. "If we get Samson, he'll never see the light of day again."

"If you get him, detective. That's a pretty big *if*. He's not called the ghost for nothing."

"Who is this Ghost?" Kasey replied. "I've never heard of him."

"That's because he's new to New York," Bishop replied. "Up until now, he's operated all up and down the West Coast. I wonder what brought him to our neck of the woods."

"It was the gala job. Someone got it in his head that the gala would be a great target if he could pull it off. You know Samson's record. Once he is faced with a challenge, he doesn't back down," Kovacs replied. "The man is a legend."

"So why are you so afraid of, Wendell?" Kasey asked.

"That'll be because of his history," Bishop answered. "Wendell Samson was the commander of Seal Team Five. His unit did two tours of Afghanistan. He was a front-line operator of the highest caliber.

"Or at least he was, until he was dishonorably discharged in 2007 following an incident with a commanding officer. It's rumored that half of Samson's unit disappeared during a mission in the mountains of Afghanistan.

"If the same rumors are to be believed, they were pursuing a high level Al Qaeda agent. Unfortunately, it was an ambush. Samson escaped, but most of his unit did not. When Samson was pressed for details by his commanding officer, Samson hit him. Apparently, he punched a two-star general square in the face. Samson was discharged two weeks later.

"Next thing we know, Samson is back in the States and he's not impressed with Uncle Sam. Samson and his crew have been hitting high profile targets ever since. Armored cars, bank vaults, and jewelry stores. Nothing was safe.

"Samson was well equipped and working with experts. It seemed that a grudge was not all he took with him out of Afghanistan. Some believe his team survived Afghanistan and it was all just a set up. The balance of Seal Team Five are supposed to have made it out with enough heroin to bankroll their new business in Los Angeles.

"Highly trained and equipped, Samson and his team have run circles around the authorities up and down the West Coast. At last count, they had stolen close to fifty million in cash, bonds, and precious stones. Then when the authorities were ready to drop the hammer on them, the team simply disappeared as suddenly as they had emerged.

"Everyone figured they had simply retired and were sipping Mai Tais on a beach somewhere. There hasn't been so much as a trace of them in over a year. Kind of makes you wonder why they would even try something like this," Bishop replied as she eyed Kovacs.

"Yeah, with that kind of money, hitting the gala doesn't really make sense. Even if they got in and out clean. The risk is phenomenal, and they could just as easily hit a bank or an armored car. If they needed the money I'm sure there are easier places to get it," Kasey agreed. "And why hire a bunch of amateurs to help?" Kasey tilted her head at Kovacs suggestively.

"I'm right here, you know?" Kovacs replied. "But if I had to guess, I would say they banked on some resistance. No matter how trained a team might be, sheer weight of numbers in an open room is a potent advantage. I imagine Samson wanted the extra bodies for a show of strength."

"Makes sense," Bishop said, making a note on the file. "How about you, Kovacs? Any idea why they hit the gala? It's well outside his usual M.O."

"I have no idea, detective. You'll have to ask him that one. Samson wasn't a very talkative sort and I knew better than to ask too many questions."

"Any idea where we can find him now?"

Kovacs nodded. "Samson and his team were operating out of a warehouse in the meatpacking district. They might still be there. You will have to move now, though."

"What's the address?" Bishop asked.

"I don't know the number," Kovacs replied. "One of the others were driving. I could point it out to you if I saw it again though."

"Very well, Kovacs. You're coming with us. You ID the warehouse and we will take him down. If you mislead us or you lead us into a trap, well, naturally things will end poorly for you and our deal."

Kovacs leaned forward, his eyes wide in shock. "Going with you? You're crazy. I meant that I could point it out on a computer screen or something. I'm not going anywhere near that place. If Samson sees me with you lot, he'll kill me on sight."

Kasey's mouth turned up into a grin. "Exactly what we are counting on. We don't want to head into harm's way without some insurance. You'll make sure we get the right warehouse. Otherwise, we'll cut you loose and leave you for Samson to find."

"Has anyone told you you're a horrible person?" Kovacs asked.

Kasey laughed openly. "Yeah, all the time. I try not to let criminals' opinions of me get in the way of doing my job."

Bishop stood up. "Hold tight, Kovacs. I'll go ready the TAC team and we're going to take a little field trip."

Kovacs slumped back in his chair. "Sure thing, detective. If you're going to get us both killed, I don't see that I'm really in a position to stop you."

"On that we can both agree," Bishop replied, opening the door.

Kasey followed Bishop out into the bullpen, sliding the door shut behind her. As she did she looked at Bishop. "This Sampson sounds like a real work of art."

"He's a legend, Kasey. The police never even got close to him. Last night's robbery at the museum is the closest we have ever come to nabbing him. His jobs normally run like clockwork. This is our chance. We need to nail him while he is scrambling. If he goes to ground, we may never get another chance."

"All right, Bishop. I'll leave you to handle the TAC team. I'll head back to the morgue. Vida and I have enough bodies to keep us going all day."

Bishop shook her head emphatically. "Oh, no, you don't, Kasey. You're the only one of us that was at the museum. We need you to make sure we have the right man."

"But, I don't even know what he looks like," Kasey protested. "He was wearing a mask the whole time."

"You did hear his voice though. That's something. Stop making excuses. You're coming with us."

Kasey's heart sank. The Khan had been intimidating enough the first time. Now that she knew who he was, and what he was capable of, he was all the more menacing.

"I don't know how much help I'll be, but if you want me there, Bishop, I'll be there. Give me a minute to let Vida know where I'm going, and I'll be right back."

"Don't be long," Bishop warned. "We will be out of here in less than five. We can't afford to give Samson time to disappear."

"Not a problem. See you outside," Kasey said.

She took off through the bullpen. In her haste, she clipped the edge of a desk, smashing her thigh and spilling its contents all over the floor.

"You have to be kidding me," a voice declared.

Kasey turned to see Officer Morales staring at the paperwork that now lay scattered all over the floor.

"I'm so sorry." Kasey said as she bent down and began gathering the paperwork off the floor. "We got a lead on the shooters from last night and my feet got ahead of me."

Morales looked from the scattered paperwork to Kasey and back again. "Go on, get out of here."

"Thanks, Morales, I owe you one."

"And I'll collect. Next time we're out, first round is on you."

"You got it," Kasey called over her shoulder as she ran for the stairs.

Bounding down them two at a time, she arrived at the morgue in no time.

"Whoa, slow down there, tiger. What's the hurry?" Vida called, looking up from his examination of a balding man in his late fifties.

"We've got a lead on the shooters from last night. Bishop is just gearing up the tactical team for us to go after them," Kasey replied, panting.

Vida rested both hands on the edge of the table. "I suppose this means you'll be shirking your duties in the morgue today then?"

"Not by choice," Kasey said. "I tried to get out of going with them, but Bishop insisted."

"Seems awfully convenient," Vida said. "You jam up my morgue with more work than we can do in a week, and all of a sudden, you get a lead that takes you out of the office."

"Don't give me that. I'd rather be here than getting shot at. I've had more than enough excitement to last me a lifetime."

Vida gave an exaggerated nod. "I believe you, Kasey. Millions wouldn't but I do." His tone not the least bit convincing.

Kasey paused in the doorway.

"What is it, Kasey?"

"I see you skipped to number seventeen, when you are done with him, I was wondering if you could bump someone to the front of the line?"

Vida dropped his forceps in protest. "Unbelievable, Kasey. First you bail on me, and now you want to dictate how I do your job. You do understand what a boss is, right?"

"Of course," she replied. "You said we were taking it in turns. If I picked Mr. Mornington and you picked Mrs. Mornington and number seventeen, that would make the next pick mine, right? That's how taking turns works, correct?"

"Smart ass," Vida replied. "Very well. Who's next?"

"I'm not sure what number he is, but his name is Cyrus Pillar. He took two rounds in the chest during the robbery."

"Sure. I'll bite. what's so special about this one?"

"You'll have to open him up to find out," she replied. "I saw something during the robbery, but I want you to tell me what you find. I don't want you to be influenced by what I think I witnessed."

"Well played, Kasey. You're using my curiosity against me."

"Not at all. I'm using it to get the best out of you." Kasey laughed. "I'll be back to help as soon as I can."

Vida mumbled something Kasey didn't catch as she headed back up the stairs.

In less than a minute, she had crossed the foyer of the precinct and had slipped through the lobby's side door and out into the parking lot.

She found the lot swarming with activity. Bishop stood in the midst of the chaos, briefing a group of officers in tactical gear.

"The man we're going after is Wendell Samson. For those of you who don't know who he is, he is a former Navy Seal. He is an expert marksman and a tier-one operator.

"We believe he and his colleague are armed and dangerous, they are currently taking refuge in a warehouse in the meatpacking district.

"We are going in quiet to avoid spooking him. But rest assured, when we arrive it will be a tactical breach. Subduing an armed target in an entrenched location should always be done with extreme caution. We want Sampson alive but if he fires on us you will need to take him down.

"We have officers in the area forming a perimeter now. We'll be there in less than fifteen minutes. Keep your eyes open, and your weapons ready. If last night is any indicator, we will meet heavy resistance. Any questions?"

The assembled officers shook their head. This wasn't their first rodeo.

"Very well. Gear up, we are rolling out in sixty seconds. Anyone not in the van is staying here."

Bishop spotted Kasey and waved her over. "Kasey, you and I will ride in van one with Alpha team. Bravo will follow us. It could get hot in there. Where is your gun?"

Kasey shook her head. "Sorry, I haven't got used to it yet, Bishop. I need some time to adjust before I feel comfortable wearing it around with me. Besides, I'm only here to ID them. You guys are handling the take down, right?"

Bishop nodded. "You better believe it, Kasey. Samson's second career is about to come to the same end as his first." She turned back to the assembled officers. "All right, boys and girls, we have a mass-murderer to catch and justice to serve. Let's roll out."

Kasey climbed into the back of the lead van, and Bishop slid into the seat beside her.

Thinking of the night before and those she had seen fall around her, Kasey's temper began to flare. As it did, her mind focused on a single thought.

We'll see you soon, Khan.

CHAPTER TWELVE

$\mathcal{T}$he convoy rolled through the Meatpacking District. Each block contained several immense structures, some were relatively new. Others were decades old with faded paint and cracked glass where windows should have been.

"This is it." Kovacs shouted. "It's the one on the left, seemed abandoned when I was there. His crew were operating out of the offices in the back."

The vans screeched to a halt.

The rear doors burst open and the tactical teams dismounted. The team fanned out to cover the approach to the warehouse. Bishop disembarked behind them, with Kasey taking up the rear.

From the cover of a nearby storefront, a police officer appeared. "Are you going in, Bishop?"

"Hey, Georgiano. That's the plan. Storm the place hard and fast. We don't want to give these guys any time to react. Speaking of, have you seen the targets?"

"There was some movement in the window about ten minutes ago. Just saw the one. Not sure if he's our guy but he certainly looks the part. Caucasian man in his late forties, built like a brick wall and he seems like he's been well trained. He checks the perimeter every ten to twenty minutes, varies it every lap. Haven't seen any sign of the second suspect yet."

Bishop surveyed the warehouse. "A building this large has to have other exits. What are we looking at?"

Georgiano pointed to the warehouse's large cargo bay doors. "Well, you can see the main loading dock. Off to the right is the personnel entry. There is another out back, closer to the office, near the toilets. Stevens is watching that one, has been since we got here."

Bishop raised a radio to her mouth. "Stevens, how are things on your end?"

"No movement here, detective." Stevens' reply crackled through the radio. "All quiet out back."

"Roger that, Stevens. We'll send Bravo team around back for the breach. We don't want to give them any avenue of escape."

"No need, detective. I have it covered," Stevens replied.

Kasey shook her head. *Male bravado at its finest.*

"Negative, Stevens. There is one, potentially two, ex-Navy Seals in there. We know they are armed and highly dangerous. Bravo team are on their way to support. Bishop out." Bishop looked to the Tactical Team Leader, an officer by the name of Andrus Lucello.

Lucello took the lead. "Alpha Team, form up on the loading bay and front entrance. Bravo, circle around back and hold position until we breach. We'll breach in three minutes. That should give you plenty of time to get into position."

"Roger that, team leader. Bravo team, let's move out."

Bishop fell in behind Alpha team as they moved toward the loading bay. Kasey had to lift her pace just to keep up with her.

Lucello continued to prepare his team as they advanced. "Look alive, officers. While the vests we saw last night were duds, Samson toured in Afghanistan and is a demolitions expert. He is more than capable of rigging improvised explosives, so move carefully. Ensure your entry points haven't been rigged or booby trapped.

"Affirmative, team leader."

Alpha Team crossed the loading bay. Stacks of empty pallets littered the bay. There was also an abandoned forklift resting in the corner, from the look of it, it had been stripped of useful parts some time ago.

Gunshots split the morning air.

"Shot's fired, take cover," Lucello called.

Kasey and Bishop scurried behind the wooden pallets. The timber work was less than ideal, but the loading bay afforded few other choices.

Another round of gunshots rang out.

Lucello scanned the warehouse, searching for movement at any of its shattered windows. Like Kasey, the team leader was hunting for any sign of the shooter's location.

From her hiding place, Kasey couldn't see a thing.

"Bravo team, have you engaged the hostiles?" Lucello asked through the radio.

"Negative, team leader. We heard the gunfire and have sought cover. We have negative visual on the targets, but the shots started as soon as we tried to round the corner of the building. Shall we proceed?"

"Same here, Bravo team. We don't appear to be taking direct fire. The gunshots were definitely from within the building, but we have not seen any movement yet. Hold position. It's possible your movement was detected. We will breach the front entrance to draw their attention. Be ready to move on my signal."

"Roger that, team leader."

Lucello turned to Alpha Team. "Let's move, Alpha Team."

The tactical squad broke cover, darting across the loading bay. The team covered each other as they converged on the front entrance. One of the officers bent down and fed something underneath the front door.

Kasey's look of confusion must have been apparent as Bishop leaned over to explain. "Tactical camera. He's searching for tripwires or hidden explosives."

"Ah, that makes sense," Kasey replied. There wasn't much point going in blind when it could be avoided.

The officer withdrew the camera and signaled the door was clear. The squad member on the right side of the door tested the handle, but it was locked. A third squad member shouldered his submachine gun and swung something off his back as he stepped up to the door. It was a large steel cylindrical tube with two handles.

It's a battering ram.

The officer was close to seven-feet-tall and hefted the battering ram like it was a toothpick. The steel ram struck the door near the handle and the lightweight door caved in. The tactical squad surged through the breach, Kasey and Bishop hot on their heels.

On the other side of the door, the warehouse opened into long rows of steel shelves packed with cardboard boxes and crates. Contrary to Kasey's expectation, it wasn't empty. At the far end of the building, the aisles gave way to a row of offices.

Alpha Team advanced.

Kasey spotted something moving. It was difficult to make out the shape through the shelves, but the blur drew her eye. Tapping Bishop on the shoulder, she pointed through the shelves.

Bishop got the hint. Raising her radio, Bishop called to the team leader. "Lucello, we've spotted movement to our right."

Three members of Alpha squad peeled right while one maintained a lookout on the offices at the end of the corridor.

At the end of the steel aisle, a shape emerged.

"Drop your weapon and place your hands behind your head," Lucello shouted.

"Easy guys, it's just me," a voice calmly replied. Officer Stevens stepped out into full view. "I heard the gunshots and came to help."

"Stevens!" Bishop shouted. "You could have been shot. Who's watching the door?"

"Um." Stevens responded nervously. "I just came through it and there wasn't any sign of anyone."

Bishop shook her head, her brow creased with worry. "Get out front with Georgiano and wait for us to clear the building. The last thing we need is to lose a man to friendly fire."

Stevens nodded and hurried out the front door.

Lucello signaled the advance. "Be advised, Bravo Team, your door is open. Stevens is inside. Advance and seal off the perimeter."

"Roger, team leader. We're advancing."

Alpha Team swept forward, scanning the aisles and warehouse as they went. The gunshots had ceased, and the warehouse was eerily quiet but for the sound of the tactical squad's boots as they struck the painted concrete.

The stillness of the situation bothered Kasey. After the commotion at the gala, she had expected more activity, particularly in light of the earlier gunfire.

Her pulse quickened as the tactical squad approached the offices. The blinds were drawn, and the offices remained dark. The only door that led to the offices, was closed.

"Alpha Team, let's clear these offices. That door would be the perfect place for an ambush. Alvarez, ready a flash bang. We go on three."

One of the tactical squad drew a small cylindrical grenade from a pouch on his belt.

Lucello held up his fingers as he counted.

One. Two. Three.

The squad member threw the flash bang through the glass pane of the office window. The glass shattered, and the grenade fell to the floor inside the office. The tactical squad turned away from the window. Kasey followed suit, facing away and blocking her ears with her palms. She squeezed her eyes shut.

The flash bang exploded with a deafening roar. A white flash rolled through the warehouse. Even with her eyes closed, Kasey could see the glare as it flared outward.

When Kasey regathered her senses, the tactical squad had already breached the offices. The last of the tactical team disappeared into the rooms beyond.

Lucello's voice reported over the radio. "We have one down in here. Two shots. He's already dead." Moments later, Lucello's voice continued. "Second office is clear. We have another suspect down in here. Repeat, we have two suspects down. It looks like someone beat us here. Their equipment matches the description from the heist last night, but we'll need Kasey to confirm they are our guys. The room is clear. Come on in."

Kasey and Bishop entered the offices. The smoke from the flash-bang was still dissipating as they entered.

Bending over the first body, Kasey found it slumped face down on the office floor, blood pooling beneath it. The wounds were fresh, perhaps minutes old.

That must have been the shots we heard when we arrived.

He'd been shot once in the back and once in the back of the head.

"He certainly wasn't expecting that," Kasey stated.

"You think it was a double cross?" Bishop asked.

"Perhaps. Let's get a better look at his friend."

Kasey moved into the adjoining office. The second suspect was lying on his back. A partially open duffel bag lay beside him. Kasey stooped down to check the duffel. The bag was stuffed with rolls of cash wrapped in rubber bands.

"Wow," Kasey exclaimed. "Bishop. I imagine you'll want to get that into evidence. Must be close to half a million dollars in there."

"I wonder where it came from?" Bishop asked standing over her. "I thought you said they left empty handed from the gala?"

"They sure did. Their bag man was gunned down in the middle of the hall," Kasey said. "I have no idea where this came from.

"It could be a go bag," Bishop replied, picking up the bag. "Sometimes thieves will stockpile some cash in case they need to leave in a hurry. Perhaps this was Samson's."

"Speaking of, I assume this is Samson," Kasey said as she bent over the body.

The build matched her memory of the Khan from the night before, but without hearing his voice, she couldn't be sure.

He too had taken two rounds, though not nearly as cleanly as his colleague in the front office.

She reached for his throat to check his pulse.

Samson's eyes opened, and he grabbed Kasey's forearm.

"Traitor..." he groaned.

Kasey screamed in surprise as she tumbled backwards, landing flat on her butt.

Samson was struggling to maintain his strength. "The traitor... double crossed me...after all we've been through."

"Is that why you shot him in the head?" Kasey asked.

Samson's face contorted. "What? No, I didn't even have time to draw my weapon. Two tours of Afghanistan and I get shot in the back."

"I don't understand," Kasey replied. "The cash is still here, my partner has it. Your friend is dead in the front office."

"Not… possible," Samson wheezed. Then without warning Samson went still.

Kasey waited for him to move again, but he was quiet. She crept forward and checked his pulse. Nothing.

Turning to Bishop, she shook her head, "He thinks his friend killed him. But that's not possible. Whoever shot our first suspect, did so from behind. If it wasn't Samson, someone else must have got the drop on them both."

Bishop began, "But we were right outside. No one else could have got in, except…"

"Stevens!" Kasey finished the thought. "He was already inside when we breached."

Bishop raised the radio. "Georgiano, is Stevens with you?"

"Negative, detective. Stevens is watching the vans. He sent me to retrieve our squad car."

The vans! Kovacs was still cuffed inside the van.

Bishop must have reached the same conclusion. She was back on the radio. "Return to the vans, Georgiano. You are to keep an eye on the prisoner. I repeat, return to the vans at once."

"But…"

"No buts, Georgiano. Stevens has been compromised, he was in the warehouse when we entered. Both targets were found dead when we breached. It must have been him. You are to watch the prisoner until we relieve you, am I clear?"

"Yes, detective."

"If Stevens draws his weapon, shoot him."

Whatever doubts Georgiano had about his orders, he kept them to himself.

"Secure the scene, Lucello," Bishop shouted as she ran for the front door. Kasey took off after her.

They had scarcely left the offices when the shots rang out.

"Shots fired," Georgiano's voice called over the radio.

"Do you have eyes on the vans?"

"Negative," Georgiano called. "I am just reaching the loading bay now."

Kasey overtook Bishop, her heart pounding as she reached the door to the warehouse.

"There's no one here," Georgiano called over the radio. "Kovacs is dead. He's been shot twice."

Bishop stopped, and Kasey ran straight into her.

"Sorry," Kasey said as she struggled for breath.

"Don't worry about it." Bishop began pacing back and forth in the aisle. "What are you playing at, Stevens?" Her voice was almost a whisper.

Bishop raised her radio and jammed down on the transmit button so hard, Kasey worried the entire radio might shatter. "Georgiano, put out an all-points bulletin for Stevens. He's going to have a hell of a lot to answer for."

The radio crackled to life. "No need, detective. Bravo Team here. We've secured the exit and found Stevens. He's unconscious."

CHAPTER THIRTEEN

*K*asey looked at Bishop. Her mouth was agape and yet she couldn't get a word out.

"Come again, Bravo?" Bishop called.

"He's unconscious. We found him slumped behind some boxes. He's still breathing but we have not been able to rouse him. I suspect he's been drugged."

"Not possible," Bishop replied. "We saw him inside only a moment ago."

"And I saw him out front, less than two minutes ago," Georgiano chipped in over the radio. "I don't know what to tell you, Bishop. We secured the exit as instructed and found him out cold. We've had him in hand for at least two minutes, maybe longer."

"Why didn't you say anything?" Bishop demanded.

"You were breaching the offices. It's the single most dangerous point in any operation. I thought it unwise to distract you while you were storming a room filled with armed hostiles."

Kasey bit her lip. If Bravo Team was correct in their timing, the man they had seen inside the warehouse could not have been Stevens.

How is that possible?

Kasey thought back to the encounter inside the warehouse.

Steven's had his hands up but had been looking at the ground. Kasey really hadn't got that great a look at him. He'd been all too eager to leave as Bishop had directed.

"Bishop. Is there any chance it may not have been Stevens inside? I didn't get a great look at him. I just saw the uniform and assumed it was him."

"It's possible," Bishop admitted leaning on the van. "I'd like to think I would have noticed if it were someone else. Doesn't explain the uniform though."

"You're right. He was definitely wearing an NYPD uniform," Kasey said pacing back and forth. "Bold as brass though, whoever it was. He was willing to drug an officer and sneak into a warehouse with two heavily armed killers."

"You think he's the one who got the drop on Samson?" Bishop asked.

"It's possible. Samson certainly seemed to think he'd been shot by his buddy, but I find that extremely unlikely based on how we found the scene. His friend was shot in the back of the head. Almost certainly before Samson was shot but we'll need ballistics to confirm it for us. We have to get these bodies and evidence back to the lab."

Bishop shook her head. "I can't believe it. Less than an hour ago we had a talking witness in custody and a lead on the Khan. Now all we have left is three bodies, and a phantom shooter we didn't even know was involved until he offed the Khan and our only witness.

"How do we explain this to the chief? We just tell him we let some guy playing dress up get the better of us? I don't think so. We need answers."

"Get me back to the lab and give me a few hours," Kasey said, anxious to take a closer look at Samson and his companion. The crime scene made no sense at all and she wanted answers. "I'll work out what happened here."

Bishop nodded. "It will have to do, I guess. Alpha Team, Bravo Team, bring us the bodies. We're heading back to the station."

"What about Stevens?" Bravo team asked.

"If he's not walking, toss him over your shoulder. We're not leaving him here."

"Roger that."

Kasey couldn't help but feel a pang of guilt for Kovacs. They had promised him they would keep him safe. In their haste to take down Samson, they hadn't counted on any other threats.

Just like the gala. There is something else going on here.

She had to get to the bottom of it.

The ride back to the station was a quiet one. No one quite knew what to say about the raid. Stevens remained unconscious and was dropped off at the hospital.

Still not completely sure what had happened in the warehouse, Bishop left two of Bravo Team to watch Stevens. He would have a lot to answer for when he woke up.

The Tactical Team unloaded the vans. The three thieves, including Kovacs, had all been placed in white body bags.

Kasey pointed to the body bags. "Can you give us a hand to get these three down to the morgue. We need to see what evidence we can get off them."

Bishop hefted the duffel bag full of cash out of the van. "Lucello, get this to evidence, would you? We'll need to see if we can trace any of it." She handed the bag to Lucello, but a roll of cash slipped out of the bag. Scooping it up Bishop set it back in the duffel.

"Come to think of it maybe we'll zip that up first." She bent down and zipped up the bag. "Thanks, Lucello. Great work today."

"Sorry it didn't end as you'd hoped, Bishop. At least it's the bad guys in the bags and not us."

Bishop nodded. "Yeah, let's hope the chief agrees with your assessment. We'll head up to visit him first. Better we find him than we wait for him to come looking for us."

"Us?" Kasey asked. "I thought I'd head down to the morgue and help Vida. He's backed up and could use a hand, I'm sure."

"He'll still be there when we're done, Kasey. We acted on Kovacs intel. Time to face the music."

Kasey sighed. "Fine. Let's get this over with."

Together they rode the elevator to the fourth floor.

Katherine, the chief's personal assistant, greeted them as they stepped out of the lift. "Hi Bishop, Kasey. What can I help you with?"

"We're here to see the chief. Is he in?"

"He is." Katherine looked up from her keyboard. "Is he expecting you?"

"No," Bishop said, "but we have an important update on the gala shootings. He'll want to hear it before he next does battle with the press."

"Very well." Katherine picked up the phone and pressed the intercom. "Chief, Bishop and Kasey are here to see you." She nodded and set down the receiver. "You can head in. The chief will see you now."

Bishop pushed open the glass panel door and stepped into the chief's office. Kasey followed her in and shut the door behind her.

Chief West was difficult to read. He was famous for his down-the-line approach to dealing with crime. He was as straight as they come and expected the same from his officers. The reputation of the fighting Ninth had been hard won and the chief fought daily to ensure it remained untarnished.

Unexpectedly, the chief's mouth widened into a smile. "I see you got them. Nice work, detective. You too, Kasey."

"Chief?" Bishop replied, raising an eyebrow as she took her seat.

Kasey slid into the chair closest to the door.

"I understand you took a tactical team after the remnants of last night's robbers. I saw your teams unloading from my window. Three body bags, it Certainly looked like you got your men, though from that look on your face, I'm starting to worry that I might be mistaken."

"Well," Bishop began, "we interrogated the suspect in our custody, a lowlife by the name of Kovacs. Turned out he had been recruited onto a crew to fill out numbers. The gala was an ambitious target and the thieves wanted a few extra men to fill out their ranks. It took us some time, but we cracked him. He gave us the Khan's identity and the location of their rendezvous point."

"Well done. Anyone we know?" West asked.

"Wendell Samson," Bishop replied.

West's eyes went wide. "Samson? Are you sure?"

"Positive. He's in a bag in the morgue as we speak."

"That's fantastic!" West slapped his desk for emphasis. "Well, that explains the hit on the gala. Samson has balls the size of Boston."

"Not that it helped him. He's dead," Bishop said wringing her hands.

"We took down Samson and all our boys came home? No casualties?"

"Not on our side, chief. We have one in the hospital incapacitated. I'll get to that in a minute," Bishop replied.

"You took down Wendell Samson without a single casualty? How is it that you aren't ecstatic, Bishop? He's the most wanted man on the West Coast, and we didn't even know he was in town."

Bishop leaned back in her chair. "No one did Chief. It appears he came cross country for the gala hit. We just got lucky."

"Why the long face detective? Sometimes you just have to take your win and move on."

"Because it wasn't us that got him," Kasey piped in.

Chief West turned to her. "What?"

"There was another shooter on site. We were not aware of him when we arrived. As we unloaded, there were gunshots. So we entered and proceeded to clear the warehouse. When we reached the targets, one was dead and the other, Samson, expired moments later. With us inside the warehouse, the shooter somehow managed to get around us and kill Kovacs, our witness, as well."

"One person took down all three suspects, including the one you had in custody?" West asked.

"Yes, chief, although I am embarrassed to admit it. We are trying to track the shooter now, but so far we have no leads," Bishop confessed smoothing her pants as she spoke.

"You think it's connected to the gala?"

"Perhaps. We've accounted for all the thieves present last night. Of the two that we captured, one died in hospital this morning and Kovacs was shot on the raid. With Samson and his colleague dead, that is everyone," Bishop replied. "Everyone but our warehouse shooter."

"Hmm." Chief West mused. "I wonder who our mystery man is then. Perhaps a relative of one of last night's victims. They are the one percent. It wouldn't be unheard of for them to try and take justice into their own hands. That kind of money can buy a lot of muscle."

"Perhaps," Bishop agreed. "Whoever it was, they were good.

Moved like a ghost. The fact they left the money there gives credence to that theory."

"Money?" West asked.

"Yeah," Kasey answered, "we found a duffel bag filled with rolls of cash. We didn't get to count it, but it could be as much as half a million dollars."

"And the shooter left it on site?"

"Indeed," Bishop replied. "The bag was open next to Samson. Cash was on display. The shooter can't have missed it."

"That is strange. At this rate it may remain a mystery," Chief West concluded.

"Not for long," Bishop replied. "I intend to get to the bottom of it."

"That won't be necessary, Bishop."

Bishop's jaw dropped.

"I'm closing the case. Samson and his crew hit the gala and killed twenty-two people in the process. By your own admission, Samson and his crew are now dead. We have no leads on this rogue shooter and we are being crucified in the press. Every day this wears on, the public loses faith in us and our ability to keep them safe.

"If we close this case today, having taken down Samson's entire ring, we will not only send a message to those who might try something like this in the future, but we will also reassure the public that the NYPD are here to keep them safe. There is more at stake than taking down a single vigilante gunman that killed a few murderers."

Bishop was stunned. "But..."

"No *buts*, detective. We'll be releasing a statement within the hour."

"Chief..." Kasey began.

"I said no *buts*, Kasey, that includes you as well."

"Chief," Kasey protested, "I was at the gala and there's more to the robbery than there appears."

"What do you mean?" he replied.

"I mean that someone took advantage of the robbery to get away with murder!" Kasey answered.

West looked at Bishop with a raised eyebrow. "What is she talking about?"

Kasey didn't give Bishop a chance to answer. "What I'm saying is that when the shooting started, I saw one of the staff kill one of the guests. The victim's name is Cyrus Pillar. He's in the morgue right now.

"Vida is conducting the autopsy and I suspect that when he is through, what he finds will validate my account."

Chief West leaned back in his chair. "So, you mean to tell me that in the middle of a mass shooting at one of New York's most prestigious events, somebody took advantage of a tragedy to settle a score?"

"That's exactly what I'm saying," Kasey replied. "I saw it clear as day. When the shooting started, one of the waiters drew a gun and shot Cyrus. It was not an accident. It was an execution.

He was standing over Cyrus, and shot him in the chest, twice. I'm telling you the waiter killed Cyrus. We may have solved the robbery gone wrong but there is still a murderer walking the streets."

"Can anyone else corroborate your account of the events?" West asked.

Kasey shook her head. "No, the other guests at the gala seem to have been too distracted. They were running for their lives. I know what you're thinking, chief, but I also know what I saw."

"But why wait until now to bring it up? Why didn't you say something last night? We spoke at the gala, Kasey," West said.

Kasey took a deep breath and tried to calm her fidgeting hands. "I was worried you wouldn't believe me. With all that I've been through, I thought you would think I was crazy or overtired. Then there was the fact it happened in the middle of the tragedy at the gala. I knew there was no way that one murder was going to take precedence over a mass shooting that killed two dozen people. I knew the department wouldn't want to divert any resources away from the manhunt."

"Well," West answered, "the manhunt is over, and the case is closed. I will be putting out that statement shortly."

"Can we at least pursue the waiter?" Kasey asked.

"Kasey, I know it was me that canceled your leave to deal with the gala fallout, but you have been through a lot lately. Perhaps with the stress of the past few weeks, you confused what you saw. In the midst of that carnage, can you really say for sure?

"It would have happened so fast. Perhaps you were just at the wrong angle and the waiter was actually shooting at the thieves. Who knows? If no one else saw what you saw, I'm inclined to think that you've just been under too much pressure. You are only human, after all"

"So, what, I'm hallucinating?" Kasey grabbed the edge of the desk with both hands.

"Easy, Kasey. Don't forget for a moment that I'm your boss and the head of this precinct. If there are any more outbursts or insubordination in my office, your time here will be at an end." He leaned back in his chair. "I'm willing to give you the benefit of the doubt, but I'll not keep this case open indefinitely chasing shadows."

"Then, please, at least give Vida a call and ask him about the autopsy," Kasey pleaded. "If nothing is out of the ordinary, I'll give up, I swear. But if he's found something, please let us chase this lead down."

West slowly nodded. "Very well, Kasey. I accept those terms. If the slugs Vida pulls out of Cyrus match the thieves' weapons, then I'm going to reinstate your leave. Two weeks, starting today. I'll not have you suffering a nervous breakdown on our account."

Kasey squirmed uncomfortably in her chair. On the one hand, the suspension would give freedom to pursue the organization that had been hunting her.

On the other hand, it would deny her the resources of the NYPD in hunting down the waiter. She couldn't let a killer run free. Plus, since Cyrus was the head of the ADI, she couldn't help but feel his murder was part of a larger plot.

"Deal, chief. If the bullets don't match, you let us run down the lead, wherever it takes us. But if they do, I'll take the two weeks and take that rest."

"Deal," the chief replied. "Let us see what the good doctor has for us." He picked up his phone and dialed a number.

"Patch me through to the morgue, please." The chief tapped his fingers on his timber desk. "Doctor Khatri, just a moment. Let me put you on hands-free." He sat down the phone and pressed a button. "How are you, Doctor Khatri?"

"Up to my ears in bodies, chief. How are you?" Vida's voice bounced around the small room.

"Well enough, doc, given the circumstances."

"We've certainly seen better days, that's for sure," Vida said. "What can I do for you, chief? It's not often I hear from you directly."

The chief looked at Kasey and then at Bishop before he began. "I'm here with Kasey and Detective Bishop. Kasey has given me an interesting narrative of last night's events. We were wondering if you have found anything noteworthy in your examinations today?"

"Well, chief, when Kasey insisted I take a look at Mister Pillar, I was a little curious. I had no idea why she was so fixated on this one. From all the victims, he is arguably the least remarkable of the lot. Certainly, in terms of net worth, that is true. As far as I can tell, he's a part of the Ainsleys' security detail, or at least he was until last night."

Kasey's mind was racing. She knew Cyrus was the head of the ADI—Arthur Ainsley had told her as much—but she hadn't been ready for his cover identity. It took a moment for Kasey to process the statement.

"But Kasey insisted," Vida continued, "so I dug around a little and found a few interesting tidbits."

"What did you find?" the chief asked, his rising tone showing his impatience.

"Well, the cause of death was of course being shot twice in the chest," Vida summarized. "The entry point and trajectory of the bullets was a little strange."

"How so?" Bishop asked leaning forward over the phone.

"Well, Bishop, the trajectory of the bullets indicate that Cyrus was shot from an elevated position as the entry point for both rounds is far higher on his chest than where the bullets lodged."

Kasey jumped on the opening. "Just to be clear, Vida, you are saying that if the victim was sitting against a table for cover and the killer stood over him and shot him it would produce the wounds that you have just described. Is that correct?"

"Indeed, and if he was sitting behind the tables, that would have made it difficult for any of the thieves to shoot him in the chest. If they had, the bullets would have entered through his back. Taken together, it means Cyrus was likely shot by someone on his side of the barrier that was formed by the tables."

"That's exactly what I said," Kasey shouted.

The steady tapping of Chief West's fingers increased in pace. "Tell us about the bullets, Vida. What weapon did they come from?"

"When I drew them out, I was quite surprised to find that they were a pair of 9mm slugs."

9mm bullets. Kasey thought. *The same type of rounds fired by the MP5.* Kasey looked at the ground in disappointment.

Chief West seized on the detail. "So, the slugs found in Cyrus are consistent with the guns the thieves were firing? They were with MP5s, if I'm not mistaken, and the MP5 fires a 9mm around last time I checked."

There was an awkward pause at the other end of the line before Vida continued.

"Chief. At first, I jumped to that same conclusion too. But Kasey's comments about the victim forced me to dig a little deeper. Using some preliminary tests on a number of the bullets we have retrieved from the victims and comparing them to those taken out of Cyrus, it seems improbable that they were fired by the same weapon."

"Well, there were many present, Doctor Khatri. We would expect some variation surely."

"Indeed, chief, but the markings are not consistent with the weapon type either. The markings on the bullets that killed Cyrus Pillar are far more consistent with a 9mm handgun such as the Glock 19, Sig P226, or a Walther P99. Not those of an MP5 submachine gun. The MP5 has a far longer barrel than a pistol and as such, the markings on the bullets form a different pattern."

"You're sure, Vida?" the chief asked, dispensing with any formality

"As sure as I can be, chief. I have run the test twice now."

"Meaning?" Bishop asked.

"You have a murder," Vida replied. "This one was not an accident."

CHAPTER FOURTEEN

Kasey leaped from her seat. "I told you so!"
Chief West's eyes narrowed at her.

"Sorry, chief," Kasey replied as she sat down sheepishly.

Chief West looked down at the phone. "Vida, thanks for the update. I need you to keep that particular piece of information to yourself. Publicly the case will be closed. Bishop and Chase will run down the lead from Mr. Pillar.

"In the meantime, all the thieves have been apprehended, so I will need you to process the victims' bodies as promptly as possible. We need to get them back to their families."

"Understood, chief," Vida said through the phone. "I'll carry on as swiftly as I can."

"Thanks, Vida." The chief ended the phone call.

An awkward silence descended on the office. Kasey felt vindicated at Vida's discovery. It meant her vision was accurate; events had transpired exactly as she had seen them. Her gift was sharpening and becoming more finely tuned each day.

Chief West cut through the silence. "You two need to move fast. We can't devote too much more manpower to the gala shooting."

"Chief, didn't you hear Vida?" Bishop protested on Kasey's behalf.

Chief West held up his hand for silence. "Of course I did. I'm not deaf. As I said, we are closing the case on the gala heist. The thieves are all dead and there is no point keeping the city in suspense. I will be going ahead and issuing a statement to that effect shortly.

"On the murder of Mr. Pillar, run down your lead, quickly. You saw a waiter shoot Cyrus. Well, that's a homicide and solving those is what we do. See what you can find, but under no circumstances is word of the ongoing investigation to make it out of this station."

"Thanks, chief," Kasey said

"If there's something to find, we'll find it," Bishop added.

"I wouldn't expect anything less. You're dismissed."

Kasey and Bishop rose from their chairs and excused themselves. Kasey opened the door and Bishop stepped out into the hall.

As Kasey went to leave, Chief West called out, "Kasey?"

Kasey turned. "Yes, chief?"

"Two things." West answered, holding up two fingers. "First, don't take my comments today personally. I think you've done remarkably well here, even under trying circumstances."

"And the second, chief?" Kasey asked.

"Second, remember this is my house. What I say goes. Don't ever forget it. If you speak to me like that again, I'll terminate your placement here. Am I understood?"

"Yes, chief," Kasey replied nodding before she ducked out of the room.

Bishop was waiting in the elevator, one hand holding the door.

"Thanks," Kasey said, stepping into the elevator. "Where to from here?"

Bishop punched the button for the bullpen, and the elevator whirred to life.

"We start with the waiter. He is the only concrete lead we have. You saw him shoot Cyrus at the gala. Ballistics has confirmed it. I'll run him down in our database. In the meantime, head down to lab and give Vida a hand. See if you can get anything off of Samson. We need a lead that will tell us what his endgame was."

"End game?" Kasey asked.

"Yeah. This whole thing is a mess. We have more questions than answers, but the thing that bothers me about Samson is that we have a tier one operator that was gunned down like he was nothing. No one has even come close to catching him before—he and his team were ghosts—and yet we find him bleeding out next to half a million in cash. He had the skills and the resources, so why was he still in the warehouse? What were they waiting for? It doesn't make sense. They should have already been gone."

Kasey nodded. "I see your point. We'll start with Samson. He is at the heart of this case. Maybe his body will tell us what we've missed so far."

The elevator dinged, and the doors parted.

"Sounds good. I'll come grab you as soon as we have a lead on the waiter," Bishop said as she stepped off the elevator.

The doors closed, and Kasey rode the elevator down to the morgue. When the doors parted, she made her way down the hall. Vida was standing in between two of the morgue's examination tables.

"We are in serious danger of running out of space!" Vida stated as he turned to face her. "I mean, we are used to being busy, but ever since you arrived, this place has turned into Central Station. I can't keep up with the sheer level of mayhem that seems to follow you wherever you go."

Kasey moved gingerly toward him. "Easy, boss. Last week it may have been me the killer was after, but the attack on the gala had nothing to do with me. You can't keep blaming me for every misfortune in the city."

Scanning the morgue, she spotted two bodies lying on the steel examination table: Samson and his last team member.

"These ones aren't mine, either. Just so we are clear. It seems the cash caused a little trouble in paradise. When we found Samson, he was still breathing. He seemed to think his buddy turned on him for the payday. It was a shame he expired before we could get anything else out of him."

"You say they turned on each other, but that's where it all gets interesting," Vida said. "Neither of their guns had been fired. I have checked both the primary and secondary weapons. All of them were signed into evidence freshly cleaned, oiled, and with full magazines. Whatever happened in the warehouse, they didn't do this to each other."

"So, you believe another shooter got them both?"

"It certainly looks that way. Someone beat you to the punch." He bent over Samson's body.

"Not by much," she countered. "We were about to breach when we heard the shots. Whoever he was, he was bold as brass. Willing to go after Samson while the police were closing in. He was dressed like a cop too. We thought it was Stevens, walked straight past us and killed Kovacs on the way out. Bishop thinks it might have been pay back for the hit on the gala. The one percent taking justice into their own hands."

Vida rested his hands on the table. "That seems like a massive risk to take. Samson and his team were facing life in prison, consecutive life sentences. Why go to that sort of trouble to kill them? Seems more likely that someone didn't want them in custody. Perhaps someone didn't want them talking."

"Oh, come on, you've been watching too many movies. It was a robbery gone wrong, not a conspiracy."

"You say that, but as Sherlock Holmes always said, 'once you eliminate the impossible, whatever remains, no matter how improbable, must be the truth.' Who else would have known where they were going to be? You only pried that out of Kovacs minutes before you got there. Whoever killed these men had better intel than you did. I'm betting on a benefactor. Perhaps they paid Samson to hit the Gala and were upset when he failed."

She nodded. "I can see your point. As far-fetched as it may seem, Bishop mentioned Samson's crew has been working the West Coast since they first emerged. A single job in New York City, it doesn't fit their profile. Why would they come out here for such a high-profile job? This heist would be considered shoddy at best. Nothing like their jobs on the West Coast. I'm told those hits ran like clockwork, left law enforcement agencies chasing ghosts. Now they are in New York dropping bodies, a lot of them, or at least they were."

Vida raised an eyebrow. "There is that glimmer of sunshine. Not a lot of damage they can do when they are on ice."

"All of them? What about the one that died in the hospital? Is his body here yet?"

"He sure is," Vida replied, pointing to the wall of refrigeration units that housed the victims. "Bottom right hand drawer. I asked the chief to request the body from New York General, just in case he could give us anything useful. I've done the autopsy, it turns out he didn't succumb to his wounds. He was poisoned. The toxicology reports haven't come back yet, but he suffered severe myocardial rupture. His heart practically exploded. You should have seen it."

"Oh, yeah?" she asked.

"Ten years on the job, I thought I'd seen everything, but I've never examined anything like that. Whatever they gave him, it sent his heart into overdrive. It simply tore itself apart."

"That much trauma? Doesn't sound like it could have been a medicinal mix-up or a clerical error."

He nodded and made his way around the table. "Not a chance. You won't find a compound that could do that in a hospital. It would have been specially formulated and synthetically created in a laboratory. It was certainly murder, and not a cheap one, either. It is likely the poison was administered intravenously through his drip while he was resting. He would have been dead before the doctors could respond to the code. From the outside, it would have looked like he succumbed to his gunshot wounds, but it was what was pumping through his veins that killed him."

She looked down at Samson. "At least now we know what we are looking for. I'll see if Bishop can get the hospital surveillance footage. I am betting whoever made that early morning hospital visit is connected with our warehouse shooter. Someone is going to great lengths to clean up any evidence of Samson and his crew. Perhaps your conspiracy theory is closer to the truth than I was willing to believe."

Vida's mouth turned to a grin. "Say that again. I didn't quite catch it."

"What part?" she replied.

"The part about me being right," he replied.

"Oh, don't get cocky. If you make outlandish claims for long enough, you are bound to get a few right eventually," she replied.

He shook his head. "Kasey, Kasey, Kasey. Sooner or later, you will learn. You may fire the opening shot, but I get the last word in my morgue." Vida peeled off his gloves and threw them in the trash can.

"I'm going to grab some lunch. I'm leaving Samson and his buddy for you. Get started on their autopsies. I'll see you in an hour."

"I'll see what I can do," she answered, picking up the scalpel.

Vida departed, leaving her to her thoughts.

She studied Samson. She already knew what had killed him. She'd been there as he'd bled out. What she really needed to know was who had killed him and why. For that, she needed a different sort of examination.

After placing the scalpel back on the table, she leaned over Samson. Seeking to channel her prescience, she focused on the mass murderer lying before her.

Show me what I need to know.

She reached out and clasped his hand.

Nothing.

Frustrated, Kasey lifted her hand and placed it on his chest.

Again, there was nothing. No mist, no vision, nothing.

"You have to be kidding me." She ripped her hand away from him. "I can't get rid of you when I don't want you, but now that I need your help, you have nothing for me?" She pounded her fist into the table, causing her surgical instruments to scatter.

Her gaze settled on the body lying on the second table. Samson's last crew member. She moved alongside the body.

"Give me something!" she said as she grabbed the man's wrist.

Still nothing. She released the man's arm and it flopped lifelessly back onto the table.

"If you're looking for a pulse, I think you'll find he lost his hours ago."

Kasey spun to find Bishop standing in the doorway, she was holding a piece of paper.

"Very funny," Kasey responded quickly. "I was, uh, checking for any tattoos or other markings. All of Samson's core crew were ex-military. Most of them have been inked at one time or another. Often the tattoos can tell you a lot about the body in front of you. Tattoos will tell you where they have been and who served with."

Bishop strolled over to the table, smile in place. "Did you find anything interesting?"

"Not yet, I was just getting started. I am glad to see you found your sense of humor, though. You seem to be in a good mood. Not quite what I was expecting after how the raid went."

Bishop's grin widened, as she shook a sheet of paper in front of Kasey. "That's because we have a lead."

Kasey's eyes went wide. "Is Stevens awake? Did he see something?"

Bishop shook her head. "No, Stevens is still unconscious, took a pretty solid blow to the head. I did, however, run down your lead with the waiter. It seems, the catering company was only too happy to give up his details. Your shooter is far from employee of the month."

"You found him?" Kasey asked.

"Sure did." Bishop placed the paper on the table. "Our waiter is one Benjamin Glassen. According to their records, he lives in Queens. Got the address and I'm ready if you are."

Kasey looked at the bodies lying before her. Vida was going to be upset, but she wasn't willing to let Ben slip through her fingers. After all, he'd killed the head of the ADI and then he had tried to kill her. She wasn't about to let that particular deed go unpunished.

"Let's go get him. Vida won't be thrilled. We've been bursting at the seams down here and I'm spending more time on the street than I am in the lab," she answered.

Bishop pat her on the back. "Oh, don't worry about that. We'll be back before you know it. I will interrogate our waiter friend and you can catch up on your lab work. It will be win-win."

"Sounds like a plan to me." Kasey grabbed her leather jacket off the coat rack. Then, she pulled out her wallet and phone from her purse and slipped them into her pocket.

Squaring her shoulders, she said, "Let's hit the road."

Bishop made her way to the door, Kasey one step behind her.

"Our new friend Ben isn't going to know what hit him" Bishop said over her shoulder.

Kasey balled her hands into a fist. *Oh, he'll know all right. Here's to hoping he resists arrest.*

CHAPTER FIFTEEN

The squad car rolled to a halt. Kasey piled out of the car, followed by Bishop, both of them already wearing their bulletproof vests.

The street was lined with old apartment buildings, the one in front of them had a bar built into its first floor. The neon sign was unlit but still readable.

"The Cracked Keg. That's certainly going to be an upper-class establishment." Kasey snickered.

Bishop glanced at the bar. "Yeah, I'm sure you'll find New York City's finest nightlife in there. Speaking of finest nightlife, this is it. Our records show Ben's apartment is on the second floor, room 204.

"Are you kidding me?" Kasey asked. "Living directly over a bar. That must suck."

"Yep, certainly wouldn't be my first choice," Bishop replied as she led the way into the building.

The apartment building had a small atrium that ran alongside the bar. A hall led off to the right with apartments lining the hallway. The building looked like it had been built in the 70's and hadn't had much work done on it since. Chipped tiles pockmarked the lobby floor. The carpets in the hallways were an old faded green shag that had seen better days.

The elevators lay at the end of the hall.

Kasey stopped as a chill ran down her spine.

"What's up?" Bishop asked.

Kasey shook her head. "I dunno. I just had a weird feeling, that's all. Just a bit of déjà vu, I guess."

Bishop raised an eyebrow. "You've been here before?"

"Not that I know of."

"Odd. Are you ready to kick this door in? The sooner we have him in custody, the better." Bishop looked from the elevators at the end of the hall to the stairs near the lobby. "He's only on the second floor. Why don't we take the stairs?"

"Sounds like a plan." Kasey followed Bishop into the staircase.

They were in the same state of disrepair as the rest of the apartment building. Worn concrete steps had been painted several times, none of them recently. Chips in the paint revealed the different layers of color, the latest being a dull gray.

Kasey followed Bishop upstairs and onto the second-floor landing. Bishop opened the door to the hall. No one was in sight.

Kasey pointed to the left at the black apartment numbers that were peeling off the wall. "Bishop, 204 will be this way."

Bishop nodded and led the way. It was only three doors down on the left. Bishop rested one hand on her weapon, and then pounded on the door with the other.

"Benjamin Glassen," Bishop called through the door. "It's the NYPD. We have a few questions."

Nothing but silence greeted them.

Bishop knocked again. "Benjamin, we need to have a word with you."

There were a series of muffled footsteps inside the apartment.

"Coming," a weary voice answered.

The door swung open revealing a bleary eyed, disheveled man in his twenties. The apartment mirrored its tenant, clothes were scattered about the room and takeout from at least two different stores were resting on the coffee table.

The young man had a deep olive complexion and was wearing jeans and a black T-shirt that bore the logo of a rock band that Kasey didn't recognize. In spite of the change of clothes Kasey knew they had found their man. The pretentious goatee was unmistakable.

"What can I do for you, officers?"

"That's him. I'd remember him anywhere," Kasey stated.

"Wait, what the...?" the man answered raising both arms.

Bishop grabbed him by the wrist. "Benjamin Glassen, you're under arrest. You have the right to remain silent. Anything you say or do can and will be used against you in a court of law. You have the right to an attorney. If you cannot afford one, one will be provided for you. Do you understand your rights?"

Bishop twisted his arm as she spoke, turning him against the apartment's wall. Lifting her cuffs from her belt, she clasped them around his wrists.

"W-wait? Under arrest, for what?" Ben protested.

"The shooting of Cyrus Pillar. Eyewitnesses saw you shoot him during the robbery last night."

"Well, your witnesses are liars. I didn't shoot anyone, and I don't even own a gun."

"Doesn't mean you couldn't have gotten one from somewhere else," Kasey asserted.

Ben shook his head. "Why would I need one? You mentioned a robbery. I don't know anything about a robbery."

"The robbery at the Met. You know the one that left twenty-two people dead including the man you shot. Don't worry, I'm sure the ride back to the station will jog your memory a little."

Ben tried to gesture with his arms, but the cuffs prevented him from lifting them. "Wait a minute, wait. You said the Met? Someone tried to rob the gala? It seems like I picked the right night to skip work. I wasn't even there, and I can prove it."

Kasey looked at Bishop and shook her head.

Ben saw the gesture and pushed on. "I said I can prove it. I was downstairs in the bar for most of the night. I have dozens of witnesses."

"You mean dozens of friends who are ready to lie for you?" Kasey interrupted. "You see, Ben, I was at the gala. I saw you shoot Cyrus and when I tried to chase you down, you took a shot at me, as well. You really think I would forget something like that?"

Ben studied Kasey. "Look, I don't know what you're talking about. I wasn't at the gala and I sure as hell didn't shoot anyone. Not this Cyrus fellow and I certainly didn't try to shoot you. I am sure I would remember that."

Kasey narrowed her eyes at him.

"I'm telling you, you have the wrong man. I was in the bar for half the night. All you have to do is talk to Carl at the bar. He'll back up my story. I skipped work. I always hated working the gala. That crowd has too much money and not enough manners. I was drinking with Carl and I decided to blow off work. I don't know what you saw, but it wasn't me, because I wasn't there."

Bishop turned to Kasey. "Look, I'm not doubting you, but the bar is just downstairs. May as well check it out while we're here. It will save us having to make a trip back."

"Fine, let's see what this Carl character has to say about your story."

Bishop grabbed Ben by the arm and began pushing him out the door.

Ben stopped and dug in his heels. "Hey, officer, would you mind grabbing my wallet and keys off the shelf over? there. I don't want to be locked out when I get home"

He cocked his head to the left, motioning at a shelf.

Kasey spotted a wallet and a set of keys sitting in an otherwise empty fruit bowl. "I've got it, Bishop." She made her way over to the bowl and snatched up the wallet and the keys. "Anything else, Ben? Want us to grab a packed lunch for you?"

"Is that an option?" Ben smirked.

"Afraid not," Bishop replied, steering him into the hall.

Kasey followed her out of the apartment and shut the door. With the lifts being at the opposite end of the hall, Kasey opted for the stairs.

They made their way down the stair well and into the lobby of the building. Soon they were on the street, pedestrians parting out their way.

Together the three headed for the door of the Cracked Keg. The large weather beaten timber door was shut. Kasey pulled on the handle, but it was locked.

"Seems like you are fresh out of luck, Ben. You can take a ride down to the station with us, until we can find someone to corroborate your story."

"Don't mind the lock," Ben replied. "Carl practically lives here. Just bang on the door."

Kasey sighed, then knocked on the heavy door.

"Hey, Carl," Ben called. "It's me, Ben. I need a hand."

There was a loud click as the door's deadbolt opened. The heavy door swung inward revealing a sandy haired man standing in the doorway.

"Ben, it's barely 2pm. You need to get a life, man." It took Carl a moment to realize Ben was handcuffed. "Hey, what's going on?"

"Hey, Carl, sorry to bother you. I just need you to explain to these good officers that I was here in the bar with you last night. I skipped work, but they don't seem to believe me. They think I shot some guy..."

Bishop interrupted Ben's rambling. "Hi, Carl, I'm Detective Bishop from the Ninth Precinct. Ben, here, assures us he was here drinking until late last night. Did you see him last night?"

Carl sighed. "I see him most nights, detective, but yes, I saw him last night. He probably left around nine. He wasn't alone."

"Oh?" Bishop asked. "Who was he with?"

"A new girl. I've never seen her before. Red head with a bit of an attitude. The two were drinking at the bar for a while before they left together around nine."

Bishop turned on Ben. "Why didn't you mention your friend before?"

"A gentleman doesn't kiss and tell, detective. I thought Carl's word would be sufficient."

"It's not," Bishop replied. "Keep talking. Who was the woman?"

Ben looked down at his feet. "Look, I don't know a whole lot about her, to be honest. I came in to grab a drink before work. Spotted her at the bar and had to say hi. She was a stunner, redhead with... well, let's say she had a killer"—Ben looked from Bishop to Kasey and back— "personality."

"Nice save," Carl chimed in.

"Not even close," Kasey said, "but keep talking."

"Well, I bought her a drink and we hit it off. It was time to head off for work, but things were going so well that I decided to blow off work and take my chances with our fiery-haired friend."

"And?" Bishop probed.

Ben flushed a little. "Well, detective, after that we blew the bar and things...well, it was a great night."

"Where did you go?" Kasey asked.

"Upstairs," Ben replied.

"You took a woman home to that mess?" Bishop asked, her face twisted into a pained look.

"No, that's the best part. Turns out she lives just upstairs, moved in last week. Skipping work last night was the best decision I've made all year."

"I saw you there. You can't lie to me," Kasey said.

Ben's face was flushed. "I'm not lying. I don't know who you saw but it wasn't me. You heard Carl, I was here."

"Your boss didn't think so," Bishop replied. "From the tone of your boss's voice, I'd say he'd have fired you for skipping work."

Ben shrugged. "No great loss. I can get another job if I have to."

"Did this redhead have a name?" Bishop asked.

"Yep, sure did, Skyler," Ben answered.

"And you say she lives upstairs?"

"Sure does. Fourth floor."

"Great. Take us there," Kasey said.

"You have to be kidding!" Ben shook his head. "I'm not going there like this. What sort of message would that send? I mean, I want to see her again, but this isn't what I had in mind."

"Well, she's your alibi for the robbery. Carl might have seen you leave together, but if she's your alibi, we are going to need a statement from her, as well. These are murder charges, not misdemeanors."

Ben was not impressed. "Fine, but I'm telling you, I had nothing to do with that. I didn't go within ten miles of the museum and Skyler will vouch for that."

"Let's hope so, Ben, and if she does, you are a free man. We won't even drag you down to the station," Bishop stated.

Kasey shot Bishop a wide-eyed look.

Bishop simply shrugged. "Two people independently corroborating his alibi, Kasey. He'll be a free man. On the other hand, if Skyler's story doesn't match Carl's, you'll be taking a ride with us."

"Fine. Let's get this over with. She's upstairs, room 406."

"Thanks for your time, Carl. We appreciate it," Bishop said over her shoulder, as she steered Ben back into the building.

With Ben between them, Kasey hurried with Bishop through the lobby. Bishop looked toward the stairs.

"Oh, come on," Ben said. "You two may like the stairs, but they put in the elevators for a reason. Cut me a break."

"Quit your whining," Kasey said as they guided him down the hallway toward the two elevators.

They stopped in front of them, and Kasey pressed the call button. The left-hand elevator lit up.

The lights on the floor display steadily wound down and soon the elevator doors parted. Kasey stepped onto the elevator, followed by Bishop with Ben. As the doors closed, Kasey had the same familiar sense of déjà vu she had experienced earlier. Shaking it off, she focused on the matter at hand. She pressed the button for the fourth floor, then stepped back against the worn aluminum wall of the elevator.

The trip to the fourth floor only took a few moments and soon the elevator doors parted, revealing a long corridor furnished exactly like the one in the lobby. Apartments lined both sides of the hall.

A steady stream of foot traffic had worn a furrow down the center of the carpet. It was the same faded forest green that had been used downstairs.

Kasey led the way to room 406, Bishop with Ben right behind her.

"Well, what are you waiting for?" Bishop asked. "Let's hope she's home."

"Oh, it's not that," Ben replied. "It's just, I haven't even called her yet. It's a little weird to show up on her doorstep unannounced."

"It'll be weirder to spend the night in holding, trust me," Bishop replied.

"Well, if one of you ladies could knock for me, that would be greatly appreciated. These cuffs make it more than a little difficult."

Kasey glanced at him, then pounded on the door

"Coming," a voice called. It was smooth and sonorous, like a singer. There was a slight accent that Kasey couldn't place.

The door opened, revealing a young woman that couldn't be more than twenty. The woman was perhaps five-foot two but had curves to kill for. It was easy to see why Ben had skipped work. Between the striking red hair and ready smile, he hadn't stood a chance.

"Hey, there!" Skyler said with a smile. "I wasn't expecting to see you again so soon."

Skyler's eyes wandered over Kasey and Bishop before settling back on Ben. "Why are the police here?"

"Hi Skyler," Bishop started. "I'm sorry to interrupt your morning. My name is Detective Bishop from the Ninth Precinct. This is Kasey, one of our medical examiners."

"The police? Am I in trouble?" Skyler asked, her lip quivering.

"No, not at all, Skyler. We have evidence that places Ben at a crime scene last night. Ben, however, insists that he spent the night here. We were wondering what you have to say about that. Are you willing to corroborate his story?"

Skyler bit her lip. "Corroborate? I'm sorry, I don't get it. What is it you are wanting me to do?"

Kasey rolled her eyes, but Bishop was more patient.

"Skyler, Ben told us that he spent the night here. We need to know from you whether or not that is true and if you would be willing to sign a statement to that effect."

"Oh sure, I can do that," Skyler replied. "He was here most of the night. Didn't leave until early this morning. I don't see how he could have been anywhere else. I am sure I would have noticed."

"Would you sign a statement to that effect?" Bishop asked.

"Of course," Skyler replied. "That's what happened."

"We appreciate your help, Skyler." Bishop reached into her pocket and drew out a key for the handcuffs. Reaching behind Ben, she uncuffed him.

"Mr. Glassen, Skyler, we appreciate your help this afternoon. The Ninth Precinct apologizes for any inconvenience we might have caused you," Bishop said gently as she released Ben. "We will send someone by later with statements for you both to sign, but until then, have a great day."

Ben rubbed his wrists. "Sorry, Skyler, not how I pictured today going. I appreciate your help."

"Happy I could, but now that you're here, want to come in?" Skyler asked.

Ben was dumbfounded. "Ah, yeah, sure."

Turning to Bishop and Kasey, he nodded. "We'll see you later, officers."

Skyler grabbed Ben by the shirt and pulled him into the apartment before closing the door.

The walk back to the elevator passed in awkward silence.

Bishop reached for the button.

Kasey couldn't take it anymore. "I know what I saw, Bishop. Clear as day. Ben shot Cyrus at the gala."

Bishop gently shook her head as the doors parted. Kasey followed her into the lift and pressed the button for the ground floor.

Bishop looked at her. "I know what you think you saw, but he has two people who are willing to swear that he was nowhere near the gala last night. Hell, there is probably a dozen or more others who saw him in the bar. There is no way that charges are going to stick until we find something more concrete. We need a smoking gun, literally."

"So, we have nothing?" Kasey asked.

"Pretty much," Bishop replied. "Samson and his band of thieves are all dead. The last of them, including Kovacs, were gunned down by a ghost who slipped straight through our fingers. Cyrus' shooting was the only killing at the gala that was executed with any degree of forethought, and our only lead was Ben. Turns out, that he is a dead end too."

The elevator doors opened, and Bishop stepped out of the lift. Kasey didn't move.

"Bishop. What if I only thought I saw Ben shoot Cyrus?"

"You think it was the thieves, after all? I thought Vida's results ruled that out."

"No, no," Kasey replied. "The person I thought was Ben. What if it wasn't him? What if it was our ghost? After all, we thought it was Stevens in the warehouse today, but it wasn't. It was the ghost. What if the same man was at the gala? What if he wore some sort of mask and took Ben's place on that shift to get to Cyrus?"

The elevator door tried to close but Kasey held it firm.

"That's a lot of *buts* and *what ifs*, Kasey. It might be a nice theory, but unless we have a way of finding our ghost, it's just a theory."

"Well, I was thinking about that," Kasey said. "Until I realized... our shooter would need to be sure Ben didn't show up for his shift."

"Exactly. Meaning he has a partner, Skyler." Bishop concluded, drawing her gun as she stepped back into the elevator.

Kasey removed her hand. As the worn aluminum doors slid shut, three gunshots rang through the building.

CHAPTER SIXTEEN

*a*s the elevator neared the fourth floor, Bishop looked at Kasey. "Careful, Kasey. Whoever wanted Cyrus dead is cleaning house. First Samson and now Ben. We brought him right to her."

"She would have gone after him either way. It was only a matter of time. At least we were here when it happened," Kasey replied.

"That's cold, and it's not like you." Bishop answered, studying Kasey, "and where is your gun? If you don't have it now when it counts, what is the point?"

Kasey shrugged. "Sorry, I forgot it. It's still in my bag at the station."

Bishop shook her head. "Keep your head down. When the doors open, wait for my lead. The hall will be a kill zone. There is no cover between us and the room. As soon as we step out of the lift, we'll be exposed."

Kasey nodded. With Bishop in the mix, using her magic was out of the question. She would save their lives only to expose the existence of the World of Magic. The Arcane Council would be furious and had already proved themselves heavy handed in enforcing the Anti Discovery Initiative.

The light on the floor display rested on the fourth floor. It felt like an eternity as the aluminum doors slid open.

Kasey's heart pounded in her ears. A trickle of sweat ran down her brow as she sought to ready herself for the cold-blooded killer waiting in room 406.

The doors came to a halt, and Bishop scanned the corridor. It was clear.

Bishop leaned forward to check the space on either side of the elevator. Both were empty.

She made her into the hall. Kasey followed close behind.

The journey down the hallway to room 406 seemed to drag on for hours, though in reality it was mere seconds.

Bishop reached the door to Skyler's apartment and raised a hand for Kasey to wait. Kasey halted in her step.

Bishop tested the handle and found it was open. Using the cover of the door jam, she pushed open the door.

Ben lay in the middle of the floor. Skyler was nowhere to be seen.

"Kasey, see to Ben," Bishop said in a low voice.

Kasey hurried over to her. Together, they moved into the apartment.

Bishop scanned the room while Kasey bent down over Ben. He had been shot three times in the chest.

She searched for a pulse on his neck but found none. "He's gone, Bishop. These gunshots, they are in an almost identical pattern to Cyrus. I think we are on the right track."

"We're on the right track but we're running late. We've just got to catch her, if we get her we can squeeze her for her partner." Bishop answered. "Let's move. She'll want to get to the street. I didn't see the other lift moving so she's probably in the stairwell. I'll take the stairs, you take the lift just in case. If you see her, just keep an eye on her. Don't break cover. If she'll shoot him, she'll shoot you."

They exited the apartment. Bishop ducked into the stairwell, and Kasey made her way to the elevator.

In a moment, Kasey was back inside it and heading for the ground floor. Worried that she would come face-to-face with an armed Skyler before Bishop could catch up, she readied her powers. If it was just her and Skyler and there were no witnesses, then magic would prove a potent last resort.

If it comes down to magic, she'll be heading to the morgue. The ADI won't tolerate any witnesses.

Resolved and ready to do what was necessary, Kasey stared at the elevator doors. Each second she waited was an irritant.

She is not getting away.

The doors parted. Kasey found herself looking at the first floor's hallway. To her surprise, Bishop was already halfway down the hall, heading for the lobby.

Kasey ran after her. As she passed the stairs, Kasey called out, "Hey, Bishop. Wait for me."

As the words left her mouth, time stood still. She saw Bishop with her weapon drawn, and a handbag slung over one shoulder. Bishop was standing in the worn and beaten hallway, with its faded shag carpet, and she knew where she had seen it all before. It wasn't déjà vu; she had actually seen it before in her vision.

Bishop turned and looked at Kasey. She was breathing rapidly, her face scrunched in frustration.

Without warning, Bishop raised her pistol, pointing it directly at Kasey.

She had seen her death coming. Unfortunately, the realization had come too late.

She was paralyzed with fear and her feet wouldn't move.

What spell will stop a bullet?

Kasey's mind raced but her body wouldn't answer.

Bishop's finger tightened on the trigger.

One thought filled her mind.

Why?

A door opened beside her.

From her right, an arm reached out of the stairwell and yanked her into it. A hail of gunfire tore through the hall. Kasey collided with the internal wall of the stairwell. Turning, Kasey found herself looking into Detective Bishop's familiar face.

Goosebumps ran up her arms. "What the...?"

"I opened the door and saw you frozen like a statue. You're lucky, Kasey. One second later and you'd be dead."

"T...thanks, Bishop," Kasey said, shaking as she ran her hands through her hair. "Did you see her?"

"No, I just opened the door and there you were. I figured she got the drop on you. I wasn't sticking my head out to be sure.

Kasey tried to clear her head. It didn't make sense. The woman she had seen in the hall was Bishop. She would have sworn it, at least until Bishop yanked her into the stairwell.

The woman in the hallway had to have been Skyler. How had she made the transformation into Bishop so quickly, and so completely? How could she have known Bishop would even be here today? A latex mask would take days not minutes to prepare. Her wardrobe too was a perfect match.

Bishop cracked the door and traded shots blindly with Skyler.

Kasey thought of Cyrus and the man who had shot him. The man she had sworn was Ben. She thought of the warehouse raid and the man they thought was Stevens. Now Bishop. The transformations were too quick, too complete, too good to be a costume or a ruse.

It must be magic.

That was the only possibility that made any sense. Cyrus was the head of the ADI. Whoever wanted him dead would have needed the element of surprise. Cyrus had been a wizard, no doubt a formidable one to have risen to such a prominent position in law enforcement in the magical community. It made sense that magic might be needed to kill him. Kasey simply hadn't expected something so subtle. She'd never seen anything like it.

Bishop reached into the hall. This time no gunshots greeted her. Bishop snuck a glance into the hall. "All right, Kasey, let's go. She's on the move."

Bishop darted out the door. Kasey was right on her heels. They raced down the hallway, through the lobby, and out the front door. The sound of the city assailed them as they searched for Skyler.

Kasey caught a glimpse of Skyler making her way down the street. There was no sign of the gun, but she had resumed the form they had first met her in. She rounded a nearby corner.

"There, Bishop, she just turned left," Kasey shouted, pointing down the street.

She ran after Skyler. Her heart was racing with each footstep. Bishop was right beside her, gun in hand.

Pedestrians stared as they blitzed past them. One of them, a young man on his phone, stared in slack-jawed amazement—until he realized he was in their way. At the last moment, he leapt out of their path. Up ahead, Skyler pressed through the foot traffic that thronged the city streets.

Kasey sucked in a deep breath and kept moving. Slowly but surely, she reeled Skyler in.

Skyler risked a look over her shoulder and then doubled her efforts. Reaching the street, she didn't hesitate as she leapt into the traffic. She weaved between the lanes as horns blared. Incredibly, she made it across the street unscathed.

Kasey went to follow her, but Bishop grabbed her by the arm.

"What are you..." Kasey began.

A yellow cab tore up the street. It would have run her down if not for Bishop.

"Careful, Kasey. Focus is good, but tunnel vision will get you killed."

Kasey nodded, and then checked the road to her left. Seeing a gap in the traffic, she dashed into the street. The traffic had given Skyler a moment's respite, but she wasn't going to let her get away.

Skyler ducked into an alley.

Bishop rounded the corner first, but Kasey was right behind her. Together, they sprinted down the alley.

The narrow corridor was littered with dumpsters and garbage. Skyler made matters more difficult by knocking over trashcans as she went. The trashcans rolled across the path.

Kasey deftly jumped the rolling receptacle and kept moving. Bishop cleared the can but landed on a loose bottle. The bottle slid, taking her down with it.

Bishop groaned as she went down.

Kasey turned to see Bishop in a heap on the pavement.

Wincing empathetically Kasey asked, "Are you ok?"

Bishop grunted as she rolled onto her stomach. "Don't mind me, keep your eyes on her. I'll be right behind you."

"Right!" Kasey nodded. Standing up, she checked the alley for a sign of Skyler.

Skyler stood dead ahead of her at the alley's exit, gun in hand, drawing a bead directly on her. Kasey dove for the cover of the nearby dumpster as gunfire lit up the alley.

The shots ricocheted off the solid steel.

She checked on Bishop and found her hunkered on the ground only a few paces behind her.

The gunfire stopped. Kasey risked a look around the dumpster.

Two more shots pinged harmlessly off the dumpster as Kasey dropped back behind it.

Click, Click.

She's out of ammo.

Kasey came out of her crouch and broke into a sprint. The move caught Skyler by surprise and before she could react, Kasey was on top of her.

With one hand, Kasey grabbed for the gun. She caught Skyler by the wrist and twisted it. Skyler's other hand was fishing around her bag, likely reaching for another magazine.

Kasey slammed the gun hand into the wall, sending the weapon skittering across the floor of the alley.

"Bishop!" Kasey shouted.

"I'm coming," Bishop called back. "I think I sprained my ankle."

Kasey glanced down the alley to see Bishop hobbling toward her. The choice cost her. Skyler's left fist arced straight for Kasey's face.

She leaned back but still caught the side of the blow.

Her jaw throbbed as her nerves shot into overdrive. Fortunately, it wasn't the first time she'd been punched in the face. Shaking off the blow, Kasey kept her vicelike grip on the woman's wrist.

Skyler drew back for another punch.

Kasey, still holding Skyler's other wrist, yanked the small woman off her feet into a crude fireman's carry. She stumbled out of the alley and onto the sidewalk before dumping Skyler heavily onto the sidewalk.

Skyler groaned as the wind was driven out of her.

A screeching noise drew Kasey's attention.

Kasey looked up to see an approaching cyclist swerving to avoid running over Skyler. His handlebars clipped Kasey. Both Kasey and the cyclist went down in a heap on the sidewalk.

The handlebar in her stomach hurt, but Kasey ignored the pain in favor of searching for Skyler.

She was on her knees, rifling through her bag. Her mouth twisted up into a grin as she drew out a knife. She fixed Kasey with a stare.

"*Shi-ne,*" she growled as she dove at Kasey.

As the blade descended, Kasey grabbed Skyler's arms, drove her foot into her stomach, and yanked her forward. Skyler sailed straight over Kasey and landed in the street.

There was a shrill screech of brakes, followed by two sickening thuds. She knew what had happened without even looking. The sound was unmistakable.

By the time Kasey was on her feet, the driver was out of the cab. He was panicking. "I don't know where she came from. I tried to stop."

Kasey looked behind the cab. Skyler had been run over. Twice.

Kasey wove around the car and then bent down over Skyler. Her chest had been crushed; she was likely suffering from internal bleeding. Her knife lay on the road, well out of her reach. Kasey had seen the aftermath of such injuries before. Skyler wasn't going to make it.

Kasey grabbed her by the shirt. "Who are you? Why did you want Cyrus dead?"

Skyler spat out a mouthful of blood. "You. Will. Die. For. This."

"You won't be alive to see it," Kasey replied.

Skyler leaned her head back and closed her eyes.

"Kasey what happened?" Bishop called as she made her way out of the alley.

Kasey shook her head. "Sorry, she drew a knife. It was her or me."

Bishop saw Skyler laying in the street. Traffic stopped all around her.

"You know," Bishop started, "suspects are much better at answering questions when they are still alive."

"No kidding. Vida's going to kill me."

Bishop's brow furrowed. "Vida? Why?"

"First, I skipped out on an autopsy to help you in the field. Now, we're bringing in another body."

"Two," Bishop replied.

"Huh?"

"Two bodies. Ben is still back there in the apartment," Bishop reminded her. "I'll phone for backup. We're going to need some help cleaning this up."

Kasey felt a pang of guilt at Ben's death. She wished she had put together the pieces sooner.

"Don't beat yourself up. You can't have known," Bishop replied, as if reading her mind. "At least we got one of our ghosts. One down. One to go. It was her partner that shot Cyrus. Let's get Skyler back to the lab and see if we can't find a clue that will lead us to him."

Kasey nodded, still reeling from the fight.

Bishop turned to address the growing crowd. "Okay, folks, back it up. Give us some space."

Kasey looked at Skyler laying in the street. "Not again. Vida's going to kill me."

CHAPTER SEVENTEEN

*K*asey stared at the body bag resting on the morgue's examination table before her. By some miracle, there was no sign of Vida—yet.

She was determined to get the autopsies underway before he returned. She could imagine the lecture already. Plus, while Vida was good natured, she still felt guilty over leaving the morgue's workload squarely in his lap, even if she had been out fighting for her life.

As she sized up the white body bag, she couldn't help but feel something was amiss. Clearly, the ghost had been a witch of some kind, but that type of shapeshifting magic was beyond the limits of anything she had ever heard of. Witches and wizards were known to use their magic to shapeshift into birds or animals, but using it to impersonate other people, that was an entirely new and unwelcome revelation. It meant Skyler's partner, the person who had shapeshifted into Ben and shot Cyrus, would also be a witch or wizard. They would also be capable of copying anyone's appearance.

A murderer that could be anyone. That's not terrifying at all.

Kasey unzipped the body bag.

"What the...?"

She didn't recognize the body in the bag. The woman's face was rounder, her eyes higher and more angular. Her complexion had paled, and it was far too early to be a result of her death.

As Kasey watched, the red hair changed color, starting at the roots, it darkened to jet black.

"Her magic is fading," Kasey reasoned to herself. "I can't risk Bishop seeing her like this. Far too hard to explain away."

She raced to the door and shut it, then thinking about the risk, locked it for good measure. At least she'd have some warning if Vida returned and tried to let himself in.

Making her way back to the table, she pulled the body bag down to get a better look at Skyler. As she lifted the woman's limbs free of the bag, she spotted a tattoo on her lower arm. Kasey turned the arm over for a better look.

A mist gathered, clouding her sight and she found herself immersed in a vision.

As the mist cleared she was staring at a cream surface. Focusing, she could make out a wall of woven fibers.

It's not a wall, it's a mat, and I'm kneeling.

She realized she was witnessing the vision from the Skyler's viewpoint. Unfortunately, she appeared to have her face pressed to the floor in obeisance.

This is not particularly helpful.

"How are our plans progressing?" a deep voice before her asked. Kasey tried to place the man's accent but could not.

"They proceed well, master," another answered.

Master. A chill ran down Kasey's spine. The title reminded her of Danilo's last words. The Werewolf had refused to identify his employer, even in death. He had been too afraid to consider it. Instead, he had referred to his employer as master.

Could these be one and the same master?

"There is no margin for error here. The time for our judgment is at hand," the master answered.

"Worry not, master," another voice chimed in. "We will kill Cyrus at the gala. We've arranged for the perfect cover. It will raise no suspicion, as he will be but one death of many."

"You will send many souls to the next life?" The master paused as he considered the answer. "That is well. The rest of this city will join them soon enough."

"Indeed, master. I have already found the server whose face I will use. Mina will distract him, and I will ensure that Cyrus does not survive the gala."

"Very well," the master answered. "The loss of Cyrus will throw the ADI into chaos. Their confusion will aid us as we bring our plan here to fruition."

"And the council? Are they suspicious?" a feminine voice added. The voice was coming from where she was kneeling.

That voice must be Skyler, well, Mina, I guess.

"Not at all," the master replied. "I will sow confusion among them until it is too late. Bureaucracy will be the death of them all."

"The council should never have defied your edict, master," another woman's voice added.

"They will soon learn the price of their folly. I am sure if any of them survive, they will be more...amenable," the master replied. "Our time draws near. Leave no loose ends."

"Yes, master," the three voices replied in symphony.

Kasey heard a sliding sound and could sense the meeting coming to a close.

Look up, damn it. Give me something.

Mina did, but the master was already gone. As Mina's eyes scanned the room, Kasey spotted the other two acolytes, their heads pressed to the mat as they affected their bows. One had jet black hair, the other blond. Each wore black robes.

Kasey took in what she could of the room. It appeared to be a small chamber. The walls were wooden frames over white wall paper. It reminded Kasey of a restaurant she had once eaten in.

"Mina!" a voice called.

As Mina's head turned, the mist descended, clouding Kasey's view once more. The vision ended as abruptly as it had begun.

"Oh, come on!" Kasey demanded as the morgue came back into view.

What good was the dead woman's name? She already had her on a slab. She needed to know the other's identities, before they caused any more damage.

And what about the master and his promised judgement? Is the judgment the attack I have seen in my visions?

Cyrus' death seemed to lend credence to that possibility. The master had said as much himself.

I need to know who these psychos are.

Kasey did the only thing she could think of. Reaching into her jacket, she drew out her phone. She dialed the number and set it on speaker while she continued to examine the body.

"Hey, hun, good to hear from you," her mother said through the phone.

"Hey, mom. It's good to hear your voice," Kasey answered as she opened Mina's mouth to examine her teeth.

"Are you alright, dear? You sound a little frazzled."

"I'm just having issues with a case at work. I thought I might get your help a little sooner this time, before things get out of hand."

"Out of hand, dear? What do you mean?" her mother asked.

"We were hunting down a killer who proved particularly adept at avoiding our investigations. It turns out she was a witch, and she was able to change her appearance at will. Each time we got close, she would simply shapeshift into another person and disappear through our fingers."

"Change her appearance?" her mother asked, a note of concern evident in her voice.

"Yes," Kasey replied. "One moment, she'd be a young woman, the next a policeman or a waiter. It seems she could become anyone she wished. I've never seen anything like it."

"There is a reason for that, Kasey," her mother said. "Using magic to assume another person's identity is against our laws. That is why such magic isn't taught in the Academy. The Arcane Council stamped out such practices more than a hundred years ago."

"What about Werewolves and other shifters?" Kasey asked.

"That is an entirely different type of magic. They are simply two forms of the same being and they shift from one form to another. They do not use their abilities to assume another's identity. You may have heard of the Faceless in your studies?"

"The Faceless," Kasey mused as she leaned against the steel counter top. "It's not ringing any bells."

"The Faceless were a cabal of wizards that terrorized New York in the middle of the 18th century. They used their gifts to assume the identities of prominent crime lords and gang members here in the city. Wearing the faces of these criminals, they perpetrated acts of violence against their rivals. The Eastman Gang, the Bowery Boys, the Whyos, the infamous Five Points Gang, and the Forty Thieves all called New York their home. These normals were blissfully ignorant of the existence of magic and already engaged in an escalating turf war.

"The Faceless set them against each other. Violence was everywhere, and the streets ran with blood. Innocent and criminal alike were swept up in the storm of death that flooded the city. The police were helpless in the face of such raw brutality and the Faceless used the opportunity to seize tremendous wealth from under the noses of the very organizations they set against each other. At the height of their power, the Faceless robbed three banks in a single week.

"Fortunately, such success bred complacency and the Arcane Council uncovered their duplicity. The Faceless were executed for their deeds and the very act of assuming another's identity or face was outlawed. It is a foolish witch or wizard that would so brazenly break that law," her mother concluded.

"Well, they aren't afraid of dropping bodies, so I doubt they would hold much concern for the Council. Nor any other law, for that matter. Is there any chance some of the Faceless survived? These guys seem to follow their M.O." she said, as she began pacing around the room.

There was silence down the line for a few moments.

"I doubt it, Kasey," her mother said at last. "The Council was not gentle. The Faceless and all who harbored them were exterminated. The Council has no tolerance for such violence, particularly against normals. They made the price of being caught so high, they hoped no one would even consider returning to those times."

"Well, that doesn't leave me with much to go on" Kasey answered.

"You said she was a witch, right?" Jane asked. "Did she use her magic in front of you? Could you make out the language she used? If nothing else, that should give you a starting point."

Kasey walked back to the table and stared at the woman lying before her. "Well, she did shout something at me. I didn't quite catch it. It sounded Asian, though. Maybe Chinese or Japanese. Could have been Korean. I don't really know, to be honest. Her illusion does seem to be fading now, though. If I had to guess, her features and complexion certainly match those normally found in Eastern countries."

"Does she have any tattoos or tribal markings?" her mother asked. "The ritualists of the subcontinent often wear their tribal markings proudly. On the other hand, it is common for Chinese and Japanese wizards to tattoo themselves with the language of their ancestors. You know that there is great power in the ancient tongues. They believe even the written word brings power with it."

"I'll take a look."

She began to search the body of the woman she had known as Skyler. Starting at the head, she drew back the woman's hair and checked behind her ears and neck. Moving down, she checked her shoulders and arms. As she flipped her wrist over, she found a series of lines forming an ornate tattoo.

"Found one!" Kasey shouted. "It's on her wrist."

"Any idea what it means?" her mother asked.

"None whatsoever," Kasey admitted. "It's complex. It certainly looks Japanese or Chinese to me."

"Grab a picture of it and run it through a translator on your phone. Let's see what it says," her mother suggested.

"On it."

Kasey snatched her phone off the counter, then snapped a picture of Skyler's wrist before running it through a search on her phone. Moments later, a series of articles and translations appeared on the screen.

"That's interesting," Kasey said as she flipped through the results. "Apparently, it means Shinigami. It's Japanese."

Her mother hesitated. "Did you say Shinigami?"

"That's what it says here on my phone. Why? Does that mean something to you mom?"

"Y-yes," Jane stammered. "Kasey. You need to destroy that body right now."

"I can't just destroy it, Mom. She's our only lead and she will be missed, you know. Bishop will expect autopsy results."

"The results won't matter if she's not alive to read them. Destroy the body and deal with the report later. Fake the results if you have to. You need that body gone as soon as humanly possible."

"What's going on, Mom?" Kasey asked. Her heart began to race as her mother's instructions sank in. Her mother was a formidable woman. Kasey had never heard her in such a state.

"The Shinigami are a Japanese coven. Witches and wizards that dabble in the forbidden arts. Murder and the stealing of others' identities are the least of their crimes."

"How much worse can it get?" Kasey asked.

"Much," her mother replied. "Translated literally, Shinigami means the 'god of death' or 'death spirit.' They are an ancient evil that has plagued Japan for so long that they have become a part of its folklore. They are believed to be supernatural spirits that invite humans toward death. If the people only knew the truth, it would terrify them. They are a cult of wizards who bring death wherever they go. They seek to harness the power unleashed when a soul and body split at the time of death. Their magic is necromancy in its most vile form. They have been responsible for the deaths of a truly incomprehensible number of people over the years."

"How have they not been caught?" Kasey asked. "Surely, the magical community would deal with them as they did the Faceless."

"They have never had the chance. The Shinigami are both careful and ruthless. If one is threatened, another is more than willing to unleash destruction on the community as reprisal. The Eastern Conclave have tried to apprehend them, several times. It always ends with a terrible toll in human lives. Now they do not even bother. The Shinigami are left to their own devices."

"Well, it seems they have brought themselves to New York," Kasey replied. "I saw a vision of them when I touched her body. There are at least four of them."

"And they are all here?" Jane asked.

"I don't know," Kasey replied. "It was hard to tell. It looked like they were in a temple or shrine of some kind. The vision itself seemed recent, so I would say it took place here. They were planning the attack on the Met Gala. It can't have been more than a week or two old, so it certainly seems like they are in New York."

"Then burn the body, Kasey. Get rid of it now!" Her voice echoed through the morgue.

"I can't. There is too much attention on me already," Kasey replied.

"When they come for their missing member—and they will—there will be bloodshed. The fact that you are in a police station will mean nothing to them. If they know she is dead, they will level the building and everyone in it, maybe entire the city block."

"Oh, come on," Kasey protested. "The Council…"

"The Council won't be able to do a damn thing to stop them. The Shinigami don't care about discovery. Their actions are so extreme, they have been deified in Japan. They fear no one and nothing. They bring down fires, floods, earthquakes, and tsunamis on those who oppose them. When the Shinigami retaliate, it's not an eye for an eye. It's an entire village, town, or city. Burn the body before they find you. Better they think she is missing than dead."

"Alright," Kasey conceded. "I'll take care of it now. I have to get it done before my boss gets back. One missing body is an accident. Two is going to be impossible to explain away."

"Ok, hun, be careful. I'll see you tonight."

"Thanks, Mom," Kasey said. "See you then."

Hanging up, Kasey shook her head.

Damned if I do, damned if I don't.

The Shinigami hadn't been reluctant about dropping bodies. They had already been directly responsible for dozens of deaths over the recent few days.

Her mother's warning about their retaliation looked more ominous with every passing moment.

Kasey took action. Raising her hand over the table, she said, "Here we go again. *Crebachu!*"

Power surged through her being and flew from her outstretched hand. An odd gurgling noise filled the morgue as Skyler's body and the white plastic shroud it rested on began to shrink. In a matter of moments, the body had shrunk smaller than half a sandwich.

Kasey scooped up the body and the miniature body bag and strode over to the medical incinerator.

As she reached for the power button, the lab was filled with the unwelcome creak of a door being opened.

CHAPTER EIGHTEEN

*K*asey stopped dead. She couldn't even breath. *I thought I locked that.* Forcing herself to move, she looked over her shoulder, checking the morgue's door. It was still shut.

Oh, no.

Turning, Kasey checked the only other door in the morgue—the one leading to Vida's office.

There in the now open doorway stood Vida, staring in slack-jawed amazement.

"T-this isn't what it looks like," Kasey said, unable to move.

Vida nodded slowly. "Oh, good, because it looks like you shrank that body like a 90's movie and are about to destroy it in the incinerator."

He pointed to the machine behind Kasey.

Kasey's world was spiraling out of control. The last thing she needed was her magic being witnessed by a normal. The Arcane Council had already cleaned up after her once, and they had made it abundantly clear that a repeat of such circumstances would be met harshly.

One problem at a time.

"Well, Vida, perhaps its exactly what it looks like, then. I'll be with you in just a moment."

Vida darted over to the incinerator and covered the button with both hands. "Hang on a minute. Setting aside how on earth you did that, we can't just go destroying evidence. We'll both be sacked."

Kasey's right hand grasped the body firmly. Her left hand pointed straight at her boss. "How much of the phone call did you hear?"

His eyes danced about guiltily as he stood in tight-lipped silence.

"Vida." Kasey prodded.

"Most of it," he answered. "Kind of hard not to, when it's on speaker."

"Then you know this has to go," she answered, reaching around Vida to jam the body into the incinerator's waiting compartment, before closing the vessel's lid.

"Wait!" he protested, covering the incinerator's power button with one hand.

"Nope." She grabbed his hand and drove it down into the power button.

The incinerator whirred to life. Skyler, or what was left of her, would soon be ashes.

Hopefully it will be enough.

"I'm beginning to get the feeling you have done this before," Vida stated as he backed away from Kasey.

She paused. "Was that a statement or a question?"

He rested his hand on the steel counter top as he leaned against it. "Statement. The other day, I walked in on you using the incinerator. You said you were just torching the clothes you were in when you found Lincoln, but I never did find Collins body. Just a pile of ashes with an abnormally high proportion of human DNA. We don't have Collins DNA on file but what's the chance that it will match the sample the hospital took when he was shot?"

If I deny it, he'll start digging again and I can't have that. If I admit it, then what?

"I'll take that as a yes," Vida concluded. "Care to explain why?"

"I don't have time for this, Vida," Kasey said as she pointed to the incinerator. "She still has partners out there killing people."

"The Shinigami?" Vida asked. "Seems like your friend was pretty freaked out about them."

Kasey shook her head. "That wasn't my friend. That was my mother."

"Oh, really?" he asked. "She seemed nice. Except for the part where she told you to burn our evidence. You know, we could both lose our jobs over this, right? Worse yet, we could go to jail."

"It would have been worse if we hadn't!" Kasey put her hand on his shoulder to reassure him. "You spent all morning complaining about all these bodies we have to process. This is what the Shinigami do. They kill people. If we don't stop them, more people are going to die, many more people."

He nodded as if he were trying to digest the information. "Your mother was talking about earthquakes and tsunamis. How do these Shinigami cause those? Those are natural disasters. You can't just make an earthquake happen."

"Well, I'm sure until two minutes ago, you didn't think you could just shrink a body, either?" Kasey replied.

His mouth opened slowly as he pondered the point. "Come to think of it, how did you do that? I've never seen anything like it. Do you have some type of shrink ray? Are you even a medical examiner? Or are you really some sort of secret government spy?"

"Don't be ridiculous, Vida. I'm not a spy," she said. She knew he wouldn't have believed that for a minute if she had tried to go with it.

"Then tell me what's going on, Kasey, or I swear when Bishop shows up demanding answers I'm going to throw you right under the bus. I need this job. I can't afford to get fired."

Kasey groaned. "I can't tell you, Vida. First of all, you'd never believe me. Second, if I do, I can't guarantee you'll be safe. Third, if you told a living soul, I would have to kill you myself."

"Very funny. You're going have to do better than that if I'm going to be fired, I at least want to know why."

Kasey couldn't afford to spend hours trying to convince him. She still needed answers for Bishop.

Seeing is believing.

Kasey raised her hand until her outstretched palm lay between her and Vida.

"*Pel Tan,*" she declared, invoking the ancient Welsh incantation.

A sphere of fire materialized over her outstretched palm. It shimmered and coalesced in the air between them for a moment before she snapped her hand shut. The flames disappeared as quickly as they had appeared.

She looked at Vida. His face had turned white, his eyes were wide, and his mouth dangled open as he struggled for words.

"What the hell was that?" he asked.

Kasey sighed. *Oh, I hope the ADI isn't watching now.*

"That was magic. I'm a witch, and I'm telling you, if you breathe a word of this to anyone, you'll spend the rest of your life in a padded cell or worse."

His eyes bored into her. "Come on, Kasey, you almost had me there. Magic. I'm sure if magic was real, I would know about it

"You're in denial. I get it, but I really don't have time to argue with you right now. We have an entire organization devoted to ensuring that normal people do not discover our existence. As a normal, you tend not to respond too well to the thought of witches and wizards among you."

"If that's true, why tell me?" He turned away from her.

She reached for his arm to reassure him. "You saw me shrink a body to nothing and toss it in the incinerator. I'm sure you would have figured the rest out soon enough. This way at least I can stop you from getting yourself in any trouble."

He faced her. "Trouble, how so?"

"You remember those two men in suits that showed up last week? The ones you thought were trying to deport you?"

"The ones that turned out to be internal affairs?" Vida asked.

"Yeah, those ones. They weren't from internal affairs. They were wizards from the ADI. The Anti Discovery Initiative. It's their job to make sure normals like you, don't ever find out about us."

"Normals?" Vida asked. "Sounds a little offensive, doesn't it?"

"You're an Indian man with a British accent in Manhattan. I'm sure you've been called worse."

"True," he admitted. "Still doesn't explain why they were here." He pulled up a stool and sat down.

"Well, one of the reasons they were here was you," she replied. "You know that hair sample you sent to the FBI?"

"Yeah, I couldn't find a match in any of our databases. I was trying to find out what sort of dog it came from."

"Well, it wasn't a dog, Vida. That's why they intercepted the sample. They came here to make sure we didn't do anything else that would raise suspicion."

"Suspicions of what?" he asked.

"The World of Magic =. We may hide ourselves in plain sight, but we still want to remain hidden. The last thing we want is a world full of paranoiacs with guns hunting for witches and wizards among them. It didn't go well in the middle ages and it won't be any better now."

"You're serious?" he replied. "Those were actual witch hunts?"

"Yes!" Kasey responded shaking her fists. "Why would I make this up? Now I need you to help me come up with a story for Bishop before she starts asking more questions."

"Okay, okay," Vida conceded. "One last question, for the moment. If the hair wasn't from a dog, what was it from?"

"A Werewolf," Kasey replied. "Collins was both a murderer, and a Werewolf."

"Shut the front door!" Vida replied. "Now you're just messing with me."

"I wish I was. Why do you think I burned the body? I had to finish what I started in my apartment. I couldn't risk you running more tests on him and putting it through our system."

"Why was he after you?" Vida asked.

She held up her hand. "No more questions. We'll deal with the history lesson later. It's the present we have to worry about."

"You can't just tell me you had a Werewolf hunting you and not let me ask any other questions. That's just cruel."

She rested a hand on his shoulder. "Later, Vida. We'll get to all your questions later. First, we need a reason to have disposed of the body. Things are just getting back to normal with Bishop. I don't want her thinking we are keeping anything from her."

"But we are," Vida countered.

Kasey spun to face him. "Yes, but only because explaining what we are up against will wind up with her tossing us in the funny farm, or worse still land us in trouble with the ADI The world of magic's law enforcement community."

Vida tapped his foot as Kasey paced. "What, exactly, are you planning on doing?"

Kasey stopped. "There is only one thing we can do. We're going to find the remaining Shinigami, and we're going to kill them."

"Kill them? Are you mad? First that's murder. Second, I thought your mother said to stay clear of them."

"She did, and it is. But they didn't come all the way to New York just to kill Cyrus. There is a bigger picture here and I'm not waiting to find out what it is."

"Cyrus? You mean the man the waiter gunned down?" Vida asked. "What's he got to do with this?"

"Cyrus is at the center of everything that has happened this week. The gala robbery was just a cover. It was the Shinigami that organized the entire thing to cover the real crime, Cyrus' murder."

"But he's a nobody," Vida countered. "Why kill two dozen people just to get to him."

"He might be a nobody in your world, but not in mine. He's a member of the Arcane Council and the head of the ADI. He is the leader of the Magical community's law enforcement arm. In the World of Magic, he's as important as they come. The Shinigami are planning something big in New York, and they need the ADI in disarray. They just didn't want to draw any suspicion."

Vida rubbed his chin. "I have literally a thousand questions."

"Not now, but soon. I'll answer them all. You wanted to know why we couldn't just avoid them, that's why. If we don't stop them, there will be more bodies. A lot more. I'm not going to let that happen."

"What do you want me to do?" he asked.

"Prepare an autopsy report for Bishop. The body was of a young woman in her twenties, went by the alias of Skyler. We don't have any other information. We'll need a reason to have had the body quarantined and destroyed in due course."

Vida looked at the steel shelves that ran along the morgue's wall. Spotting what he was after, he made his way over to the shelves and snatched a pair of face masks from it. The masks were designed to prevent the spread of communicable diseases.

Handing one to Kasey, he said, "We'll go with tuberculosis. It kills more people than almost any other. It can be contagious and will account for the body being destroyed, and the masks will give our story more credibility."

"Nice thinking," she replied as she took the mask and fastened it over her mouth and nose. "If you can tackle the paperwork for Skyler, I'm going to work out our next move."

"On it." He fastened his own mask as he disappeared into his office to prepare the necessary paperwork.

Left to her thoughts, Kasey pulled a stool over to the raised bench and sat down. She drew out her phone from her jacket pocket.

I need more information.

In her vision, the Shinigami had been meeting in a temple or shrine. It made sense. If people believed them to be the spirits of death, they would have insinuated themselves within the religious culture of their people. Using her phone, she searched for Japanese temples in New York City. To her disappointment, there were more than a dozen candidates.

She made her way down the list, looking for anything that might hint at the Shinigami's base of operations.

It's time to go on the offensive. I just need to know where.

As if in answer to her unspoken question, her phone began to ring.

CHAPTER NINETEEN

*K*asey startled so badly she almost fell off her stool.
Looking down at her phone, she checked the Caller ID.
Bishop. I guess when it rains it pours.

She took a deep breath to calm her nerves and answered the call.
"Hey, Bishop, what's going on?"

"Hey, Kasey, just wondering if you could bring me up to speed on
Skyler? Did you find anything we can use?"

"In a sense," Kasey replied, settling back onto the stool. "It's a
little complicated. Do you want to chat about it on the phone? Or
would you rather I come to you?"

"If you're done, come on up. I can't really leave the bullpen right
now. We are in the middle of a shift change and can barely move up
here. It's like all of New York decided to try their luck tonight,"
Bishop answered.

Kasey checked her watch. It was almost 6:00pm. She was going to
be late home.

"No problem, Bishop, see you soon." She cut the call and breathed
a sigh of relief. The busier Bishop was, the greater chance they had
that the body's disappearance would not be questioned to
thoroughly.

"Hey, Vida, it's almost 6:00. Time to call it a night," Kasey called.

"Soon, I'm almost finished here," he answered from his office. "Just putting the finishing touches on this report and I'll be out of here. What are you going to do about our friends?"

She stood and walked over to his office. "I don't know. I still have to find them."

Vida looked up from his keyboard. "Well, whatever you do, don't go it alone. Just wait for tomorrow, okay? No more hero business."

She raised an eyebrow. "Have you got some expertise on ancient Japanese death cults that I should know about?"

"No, not really, but then again, do you?"

She laughed. "Touché."

He smiled. "That's my point. Two heads are better than one. We'll figure it out together."

"Sounds good, Vida." She covered a yawn. "Have a good night."

"You too, Kasey."

She made her way over to the morgue's door and unlocked it. Opening the door, she headed for the elevator. Fortunately, one was already waiting on the basement floor.

Stepping into the elevator, she pressed the button for the second floor. The doors closed, and the elevator shuddered into motion.

It only took the elevator a few moments to reach the second floor. The doors parted.

"Wow!" she exclaimed.

Bishop hadn't been exaggerating. The second floor was thronged with people. More than a dozen perps sat handcuffed on a bench seat near the elevator. Police struggled to keep the chaos in hand.

Kasey made her way through the madness toward Bishop's desk.

"Hey, Kasey, over here," a voice called.

Kasey turned to find Bishop manning the front counter. She was locked in a struggle with a large man who she was trying to process. She had one of his arms pinned behind his back while another officer was taking finger prints from his free hand. The burly thug tried to pull free, but Bishop drove him back against the counter.

"Easy, tiger. One more of those and I'm gonna tase you. We can get your prints a lot easier when the spasms settle, so don't push your luck."

The perp stopped struggling but gave no audible response.

"Bishop, what's going on up here?" Kasey asked.

Bishop sighed. "The city's gone mad. Dispatch has been going crazy all afternoon. It started with a jumper on the Brooklyn Bridge. We've had three armed robberies downtown and a riot in Central Park. We can't book these idiots quick enough."

"Are you sure you want to talk about Skyler now? Seems like you have your hands full."

"I certainly do. Toni, here, is going to settle down and we're going to talk about the case. We need to round up the rest of these ghosts before they can cause any more damage."

"Agreed," Kasey replied as she leaned on the counter next to Bishop. "Did we recover anything from her apartment?"

Bishop shook her head. "Not particularly. Just some brochures about the city and plane tickets from Tokyo to New York with a stopover in Los Angeles. It seems she's only been here for a few weeks. The strangest thing was, we didn't find a single piece of ID. There wasn't a license, passport, bank statement, or even a piece of junk mail. If it wasn't for the body downstairs, we'd have no proof she existed at all."

"Well..." Kasey started.

"Oh, Kasey," Bishop began. "Whatever comes out of your mouth next better be good news."

Kasey paused. "Well, the good news is, we have dealt with the problem."

Bishop raised an eyebrow. "What is the bad news?"

"We no longer have a body." Kasey winced.

Bishop turned to face her. "What? You lost the body?"

Toni wrenched his hand away from the officer at the counter and pushed against the bench with his free hand. He slammed backward into Bishop, forcing her backwards. Bishop's face was a grimace as she strained to keep his other arm pinned firmly behind his back. Toni stomped on her foot and elbowed at her. They stumbled back and collapsed on the floor. The officer who had been conducting the fingerprinting raced around the counter to aid Bishop.

Under him, Bishop struggled to catch her breath.

Toni, now with his hands free, scrambled to get his feet underneath him. His gaze locked on Bishop's Glock in its holster.

"Don't even think about it," Bishop snapped.

Toni reached for the weapon. Kasey sprang forward.

As Toni's fingers brushed the holster, Kasey's fist struck his cheek, hard.

His head whipped violently. He collapsed unconscious.

Kasey shook her hand. "Youch, what is his jaw made of? Granite?"

Bishop rolled Toni off her, as she replied, "Perhaps. Doesn't seem to have helped him though."

Kasey reached down and offered Bishop a hand up.

Bishop took the hand and got to her feet. Dusting herself off, she spoke to the officer who had been taking Toni's prints.

"Finish up here, will you, Danetto? I think you'll find he's a little more cooperative now."

"Sure thing, detective," the officer replied with a chuckle as he reached over the counter for the fingerprinting scanner.

Bishop turned to Kasey. "You were saying?"

Kasey backpedaled. "We didn't lose the body, Bishop. We performed the autopsy. Unfortunately, during the autopsy, we discovered an active infection. It was tuberculosis."

"She was dead. What danger is tuberculosis to a dead person?" Bishop asked.

"Not to her, Bishop, to us. Tuberculosis is responsible for more deaths per year than almost any other disease on the planet. Each year it becomes increasingly resistant to the antibiotics currently available on the market. While countless people carry a dormant strain of TB, Skyler's was active and well advanced. She posed a danger not only to us, but everyone she has come in contact with. The body has been sent to the incinerator," Kasey said.

Bishop's face was downcast. "You have to be kidding me. I mean, I get it, it's dangerous but we find one of these ghosts and before we can force her to answer our questions, she gets turned into roadkill and then you incinerate her."

Kasey held up her hand. "Easy, Bishop. It's not like we had a choice. If we hadn't acted when we did, it would have been a risk to everyone at the station. The Centre for Disease Control may have been called in. Being quarantined here in the station for forty-eight hours isn't going to help us catch these guys, so I did what I had to do to keep our investigation moving."

Bishop took a deep breath. "But you did manage to get the autopsy done, didn't you? Before you destroyed the body?"

"Yes. We locked down the morgue for the duration and took precautions to ensure the infection was not spread."

"Tell me you got something we can use. We're holding on by a string here. Every time we get anywhere close to these guys, they shut us down. Did I tell you about the thief in the hospital?"

"Yeah, Vida performed the autopsy this morning, he told me the thief was poisoned. Toxicology hasn't come through yet, but it was potent. The thief didn't stand a chance," Kasey replied leaning against the counter.

Bishop nodded. "I figured. After Kovacs and the others were killed, I went to the hospital and ran through their surveillance footage. The footage shows someone slipping into his room early this morning. At a glance, he looked like a doctor, but after our experience at the warehouse, I dug deeper. I checked all the footage for that wing. At the moment the doctor entered his room, all the doctors that were on shift were accounted for in other patient's rooms or were at the nurse's station. Our suspect coded shortly after our mystery doctor left his room. At the time, the hospital believed it to be a result of his injuries. Now we know better."

"Poison," Kasey answered. "Vida said his heart practically exploded in his chest. The thief had already lost a lot of blood from the shootout at the gala. In that kind of weakened state, he didn't stand a chance."

"Precisely," Bishop replied tapping her hand on the counter. "Unfortunately, our killer was wearing a hospital mask so identifying him is going to be difficult. We have his height at about 5'8" with dark black hair. Not a lot to go on, unfortunately. We'll run the scene again, but given it's a hospital, it is unlikely anything has survived their cleaning procedures."

Kasey sighed. "Another dead end, I guess."

"Oh, come on, Kasey," Bishop replied, fighting a chuckle.

"What?" Kasey said. "I'll take my puns wherever I can get them."

Bishop pointed a finger at her. "Vida's beginning to rub off on you."

"You can't give him all the credit. I was this bad with puns long before I met you lot." She grinned.

"Puns aside, did you get anything useful from Skyler?"

Kasey shifted her weight from one foot to the other. "I'm sorry to disappoint you, Bishop. We went through her effects. A little cash but nothing of note. No ID, no driver's license, not even a rewards card. As you said, it' almost as if she didn't exist."

"And the autopsy?" Bishop nudged.

"Well, there was the tuberculosis, but otherwise she was in good shape. In her twenties, cause of death was clearly the damage caused by being run over by a car. Severe internal bleeding, broken ribs, and a punctured lung. We searched for any trace or residue that might tell us what else she's been up to. There was nothing. At this point, we're more likely to get a lead off the guns then we are off of Skyler."

"No luck there," Bishop replied. "Serial numbers had been filed off. We're checking with our sources but I'm not holding out any hope. You didn't get anything else at all?"

Kasey heard the question but didn't answer.

Her eyes were drawn to the motion occurring at her feet. Danetto had finished fingerprinting Toni and had rolled him onto his back. As the officer slipped a handcuff around Toni's wrist, Kasey saw it. On Toni's right forearm was a tattoo, a series of intricate lines running away from his wrist. Kasey tilted her head, so she could see them better.

"Kasey. Earth to Kasey," Bishop called.

"Yeah?" Kasey replied. "What's up?"

"Did you find anything else on Skyler?"

Kasey pointed to Toni's wrist. "The tattoo."

"What about it, Kasey? Most of the sorry cases we've dragged in today seem to have it. Looks like we have a new gang on our hands."

Kasey looked at the crowded bullpen and her heart sank.

He's a Shinigami. They're already here.

"Why Kasey, what about it?"

Kasey looked Bishop in the eye as she answered. "Skyler had one too."

CHAPTER TWENTY

Gunfire erupted within the station. Kasey looked to Bishop for guidance. The shots were coming from directly beneath them, which could only mean the station's lobby on the ground floor. The bullpen sat directly above it.

"What the hell is going on?" Bishop shouted over the gunfire as it raged on.

"It's the ghosts, Bishop, they're here. They've come for Skyler. They don't know she's dead," Kasey replied.

"Nonsense. You think they would storm the precinct? For one girl? It would be suicide."

Kasey searched the bullpen. Her eyes lingered over the assembled officers and the criminals they were struggling to contain. The department was stretched thin and Kasey could see now, it was no accident.

As she studied the criminals throughout the room, she saw it. Inked into the forearm of each of them. The sign of the Shinigami. The symbol of the Gods of Death, or at the least a cult of wannabes with the power of the arcane to bear out their will.

There should only be four of them. There were only four in my vision.

The thought of this many Shinigami filled her with dread.

Perhaps they are merely minions or hired guns, like Samson. In any case, they are here for Skyler, and sooner or later they are going to realize she is dead.

"Bishop, I'm telling you, these men, they all bear the same tattoo as Skyler. It can't be a coincidence that the very same day we find her, they all show up here. They're here for her, and if I had to bet, I'd say that there are more of them downstairs."

Bishop's gaze flitted around the bullpen. She appeared to be attempting to come to grips with the enormity of what Kasey was suggesting.

Addressing the other officers, she began barking orders. "Don't bother processing this lot now. Throw them in the cells. We need to sort out what's going on downstairs. Morales, Vincent, watch the elevators. If anyone comes through those doors that isn't one of ours, take them down."

Bishop's orders were met with mixed responses. As the officers began to drag their charges to the holding cells, the Shinigami disciples had other ideas.

In the bullpen, and in spite of his handcuffs, one of the mountainous suspects grabbed the officer in front of him and hurled the young recruit over the desk beside him.

The recruit flew over the table, collecting a computer screen and assorted paperwork as he went before sliding off the other side, and landing on the floor in a heap. Another criminal leapt atop the rookie and pinned him down.

"Get the keys," the thug replied as he rushed a second officer.

The four thugs sitting on the bench seat by the elevator charged directly toward Kasey and Bishop. Even handcuffed, the men posed a threat. The chance of being overwhelmed by sheer force of numbers was a very real possibility. Kasey watched as Bishop reached for her weapon and wished that she had not left her own in the morgue.

As the four men charged like ranging bulls, Kasey made her choice. Focusing on the polished floor before her, she whispered, "*Llithrig.*"

She felt her arcane gift flow through her being. The floor glimmered as the spell did its work.

The charging criminals did not see the glossy sheen beneath them.

The first of the thugs to reach it lost his footing. Crashing to the ground, he took out two of his comrades. The fourth saw his friends go down and stepped around the hazard.

Bishop drew a bead on the man's chest but thought better of it. Lowering her weapon, she took her shot. The fourth man went down, Bishop's bullet having struck him in the thigh. One of the other thugs tried to rise from the ground but was met with a pistol whip from Bishop for his effort.

"Stay down!" she snapped.

Flashing light caught Kasey's eye. One of the floor readouts on the bank of elevators in front of her steadily descended toward the lobby.

"Bishop," Kasey called. "Whoever is downstairs just called the elevator. We have to get out of here."

"We can't take the lifts Kasey. We have no idea what we'll be walking into. Might be some of ours downstairs or we might be walking straight into an ambush."

"Is there another way out?" Kasey asked.

"Fire escape!" Bishop shouted. "We just need to make it through the bullpen and out the back window."

"Easier said than done," Kasey replied as she looked at the chaos unfolding in the bullpen. It looked like the most bizarre wrestling match she had ever seen. Officers of the Fighting Ninth struggled against the press of thugs.

"Perhaps so, but I don't see much other choice. We certainly don't want to be sitting here when those doors open."

"Agreed," Kasey answered, turning her focus toward the brawl before her.

She sucked in a deep breath and let it out slowly. "Let's do this."

She plunged into the madness. Bishop was right beside her. In front of them, the prisoner still sat atop the rookie while he tried to locate a key for his cuffs. The officer wasn't fighting back and was bleeding from a wound on his head.

Bishop took one look at the wounded officer and aimed her gun. "Oh, no you don't."

She squeezed the trigger twice. The bullets struck the thug in the chest, and he crumpled.

Bishop glanced at the wounded rookie, clearly conflicted between the danger they all faced and the defenseless officer unconscious at her feet.

Kasey tapped her on the shoulder. "We need to keep moving, Bishop. We'll get help and come back for him. I can't patch him up in the middle of this. We're no good to anyone dead."

"You're right," Bishop replied reluctantly.

Kasey felt a hand grab her from behind.

Reflexively, Kasey grabbed the hand with both of hers. It was immense. She ducked under the arm and twisted it for all she was worth. The thug grunted in pain as his arm was wrenched far beyond its normal range of motion. The man's face contorted in pain. He lashed out angrily with his other arm. The clumsy blow clipped Kasey with enough force to send her careening into the wall of the cubicle beside her.

Unfortunately for the thug, her years in mixed martial arts had conditioned her well. Keeping her firm hold on his other arm, she continued twisting. The hold would have dislocated a smaller foe's arm, but the man before her was close to seven feet of solid muscle.

"You're in the way, Kasey, I don't have a shot," Bishop shouted.

Focusing her efforts, Kasey kicked for all she was worth square in the groin. The force of the blow brought him to his knees. She snatched a wooden name plate off the desk beside her and smacked him across the face. He struck the floor and went still.

Bishop bent over and cuffed him to a chair.

"That ought to slow him down. At least a little," she said.

Together, they made their way deeper into the bullpen, aiding the struggling officers wherever they could.

Gunshots rang out from the back of the bullpen.

A group of thugs had overpowered a detective. Two of them held down the man while a third thug, a short stocky guy with a mop of sandy hair, executed the officer with his own service weapon.

"No!" Bishop shouted.

The thugs turned. The stocky thug raised his stolen gun. Bishop was faster.

Her shots were drowned out by the commotion.

At the last moment, the stocky thug pulled his comrade into the line of fire. Bishop's rounds tore into the comrade, but the sandy-haired acolyte remained safe behind him. Raising his stolen weapon, he returned fire.

"Down!" Kasey shouted as she pulled Bishop behind the cover of the desk.

The shots passed harmlessly overhead.

Kasey and Bishop sat with their backs against the desk.

"We're pinned," Bishop said, panting. "If we break cover, he'll get the first shot."

"If we stay here, we are dead. We'll be trapped between blondie over there and whoever comes out of those elevators," Kasey replied.

The floor readout showed the elevator was now at the ground floor. Any moment now, it would begin its ascent. They had moments at best.

"We need a distraction," Bishop replied.

"I don't like the sound of that," Kasey answered. "I don't know that I feel like being the bait today."

"Doesn't need to be you, Kasey. Just head left and draw his attention. Throw something, make a racket, anything. When he makes his move, I'll take him out."

Kasey hunted around for a serviceable distraction. Realizing that the desk she rested against had drawers, she opened the lowest of them. It contained a series of neatly stacked case files. She reached into the drawer and grabbed a wad of folders.

"Ready," she said.

"Alright, go, go, go," Bishop whispered.

Kasey crawled left until she ran out of cover. Pausing at the edge of a desk, she banged heavily against it with her palm. The loud slapping noise was intended to draw the thug's gaze. The folders were to give him something to shoot at. As Kasey's hand struck the desk for the third time, her right arm flung the folders into the air. Paper and folders went everywhere, showering the bullpen in a confetti-like rain of case files.

The thug took the bait and a gunshot rang through the bullpen.

Bishop, who had circled to the right, leapt to her feet, weapon ready. From her new position she had a clear line of sight to the thug. She opened fire.

The first missed but the second and third took him in the chest.

"He's down, let's move," Bishop shouted.

Kasey strode farther into the bullpen. There were a dozen injured or dead thugs strewn throughout. Several officers lay among them.

Bishop reached the back window first. Flipping the latch, she lifted the window.

A bellow echoed through the bullpen. Kasey turned to see a handful of thugs emerging from the corridor that led to the cells.

"Bishop, we have company!" Kasey said pointing to the hallway.

Angry shouting echoed up the long hallway. It seemed to be coming from the cells at the end of the hall.

Kasey studied the thugs as they ran toward her. Something was not right. The thugs saw her and Bishop in their path. Bishop raised her weapon, and still they came on.

They're afraid, but not of us.

There was another heavy grunt, followed by a gut-wrenching thud. The rearmost criminal collapsed.

Seconds later, another heavy crack rolled through the corridor. A second thug collapsed.

As the ranks thinned, Kasey could see past them for the first time. Something was chasing them from the cells, and it wasn't happy. The immense shape moved through them like a force of nature. Another bone crunching thwack echoed down the hall, and another thug fell.

A navy-blue uniform was visible in their midst. Kasey watched as the officer raised his nightstick and brought it down again. The blow caught a fleeing criminal across the back of his head and he too hit the ground. The last thug risked a look over his shoulder. The officer leapt forward, crash-tackling him to the ground.

Kasey couldn't help but wince as the officer and the thug struck the floor like a freight train. The thug took the brunt of the force and before he could recover, the officer was on top of him. The nightstick rose and fell again. The last thug went limp.

The officer got to his feet and brushed himself off. He dwarfed both Kasey and Bishop. His uniform was torn and tattered, one side of his face was sporting a thick welt, and somewhere along the way he'd lost a shoe.

"Henley." Bishop breathed a sigh of relief. "Boy, am I glad to see you. You look like you've been through hell."

Henley took a deep breath. "Good to see you too, detective. I was in the cells when the shooting started. The little beggars caught me by surprise, did a real number on me. I think they cracked a rib or two."

In his past life, Josiah Henley had been a college linebacker that had been drafted to the NFL. Family tragedy had forced Henley down a different path and he'd ended up finding a new home at the NYPD's fighting ninth.

Bishop glanced up and down the hall. "They may have cracked a rib, Josiah, but I think they got the worst of it. They'll be out cold for a week."

Josiah shook his head. "They laid into me in the cell. I lost my cool, detective. One of them might be dead. Another's not far behind. This lot ran for it."

Bishop patted him on his shoulder. "Don't sweat it, Henley. They had it coming, and there are more of them downstairs."

"There are more downstairs?" Henley asked.

"Definitely," Kasey answered. "The shooting started in the lobby. That's when this lot lost their mind. We need to get out of here and get help."

"Okay," Henley replied, clearly still a little dazed. "What's the plan."

"The fire escape is the safest choice. We need to get clear of the building," Bishop replied.

"After you," Henley answered, pointing at the window.

Bishop glanced back into the bullpen, then scrambled over the windowsill and onto the fire escape.

"You next, big guy," Kasey said. "If there are any more of them below, Bishop will need a hand. I'll bring up the rear."

Henley nodded and followed Bishop through the open window. The image of the linebacker squeezing through the small space would have been comical if not for the sobering backdrop of the destroyed bullpen.

More lives were being lost to the Shinigami, and each one was beginning to weigh Kasey down.

Henley clambered down the ladder onto the landing below. Kasey swung her leg over the windowsill. She took one last look at the now eerily silent bullpen. Motion at the elevators drew Kasey's attention.

The elevator's floor readout flickered to 2.

A ding rang through the now quiet bullpen, and the doors parted.

CHAPTER TWENTY-ONE

$\mathcal{T}$he elevator doors slid open revealing six figures dressed in black. Four of them were wearing masks and carrying submachine guns. The masked assailants reminded Kasey of the thieves at the gala. The attack on the precinct was every bit as brazen as the gala had been. If any doubt had existed in Kasey's mind as to who was behind the attack, it was now gone.

The Shinigami were behind it, and now they were utilizing the same direct assault on the Precinct. Her mother's warning about their contempt for life had not been an exaggeration.

Masked disciples fanned out of the elevator, sweeping the room. Two more figures stepped out of the lift. Both of them were dressed identically, in black robes that reminded Kasey of something she had seen before.

Skyler was wearing those robes in my vision.

Seeing the deference the disciples gave to the pair, Kasey had no doubt that these were the Shinigami. Neither of them wore a mask.

What need is there for a mask, when you can change your appearance at whim?

The first Shinigami wore a woman's form. She had blonde hair and piercing blue eyes. The woman carried no weapon whatsoever, but her very presence commanded attention.

At her right hand was a shorter man in a matching robe. He was clearly of Asian heritage and carried himself with the confidence of a warrior.

"Find Mina. Kill anyone who gets in your way!" The woman barked her orders.

So transfixed was Kasey with the appearance of the Shinigami that she had neglected her escape. As the disciples streamed into the bullpen, Kasey moved to remedy her mistake.

The disciples turned on Kasey and raised their weapons, but the male Shinigami was quicker.

Raising one hand, he bellowed, *"Dete-Ike!"*

Kasey sensed the wave of power as it sailed toward her. Her heart raced as she searched for the words she wanted.

I need a counter spell.

The blast collided with her before she could act. The force of the blow blew her out the window.

Kasey screamed as she was knocked clear of the fire escape.

At the last minute, Kasey lashed out with her hand. Cold steel brushed her fingers, but her grip slipped off the rail.

Her stomach lifted as the weightlessness of her free fall washed over her.

The ground rushed toward her as she flailed frantically.

Suddenly, Kasey jerked to a halt and slammed against the fire escape.

"Ow."

She looked up to find Henley clutching her arm.

"Don't worry, Kasey, I've got you," he called.

"Thanks, Henley," Kasey managed as Bishop and Henley yanked her unceremoniously over the rail and onto the safety of the fire escape.

"What happened, Kasey? Lose your footing?" Bishop asked.

"I had some help," Kasey stammered, trying to catch her breath. "It was more of them in the elevator. Speaking of which, we need to get off this fire escape. We're sitting ducks out here and they are packing serious heat."

"How many are there?" Bishop asked.

"At least six with automatic weapons. They'll cut us to shreds if they catch us in the open like this," Kasey warned.

Bishop didn't need to be told twice. She charged down the fire escape, Kasey and Henley right behind her. In moments the three of them were in the alleyway behind the Ninth Precinct.

"What's the plan?" Henley asked.

"We need to put the word out," Bishop replied. "We can't have officers walking into that bloodbath. We need to get to a radio and raise dispatch. Let them know what is going on, have them warn our boys off. If they can send tactical support from the 5th or 13th, we'll be able to take back our station."

"We can't wait for them," Kasey answered pointing to the station. "We still have people inside. Vida's in the morgue. What if they get to him first?"

Bishop shook her head. "We are outgunned, Kasey. Vida is going to have to dig in and wait for us to take back the station."

"He can't dig in, Bishop. He's in the morgue, along with Skyler's personal effects. Somehow, these thugs tracked her here. When they realize she's not in the cells, what do you think they will do next?"

Bishop nodded. "They'll turn the place inside out. The morgue will be next."

"That's how I see it," Kasey said. "And when they do, they are going to find Vida, a few evidence bags, and an autopsy report. They'll kill him, Bishop. We need to get him out of there, before they can reach him."

Kasey turned and started down the alleyway.

"All right," Bishop replied, taking off after her. "Change of plans. Henley, head for the car park. Use the radio in one of the squad cars to reach dispatch. Get us some reinforcements but keep your head down."

"Will do, Bishop. You two take care. I'll see you on the other side." Henley hobbled down the alley.

Kasey turned back to Bishop. "How do you want to do this?"

"We can't use the service entrance. It will take too long to circle around the building. They will beat us to Vida for sure. The most direct route is through the lobby. If we slip in the side entrance we can duck down the stairs. If we use the elevators, we risk letting them know our movements. Our best bet is to sneak down the stairs, grab Vida, and get out. We'll use the service entrance and be out of the station before they can reach us."

"I like your optimism," Kasey chuckled without humor. "You make it sound easy."

"No, easy would be leaving him in there. But then we'd need a new ME and training them is just the worst," Bishop replied, setting off down the alley.

"Hey!" Kasey called after her.

"Come on, slowpoke. We don't have any more time to waste."

Kasey took off after Bishop. They made their way along the alley toward where it met East 5th Street. At the alley's end was the side entrance to the 9th Precinct.

Bishop lifted her ID card from its place on a lanyard around her neck and slid it through the reader. There was a metallic click as the lock disengaged. She eased the door open an inch so that she could steal a peek inside the station's lobby.

Kasey angled for a look of her own but couldn't make out anything with Bishop in front of her.

"We have one shooter inside," Bishop whispered. "He's camped behind the counter watching the station's main entrance. Anyone comes through the front door, they are going to have a less than friendly reception."

"Good thing we aren't planning on walking through the front door, then," Kasey said.

"True, but when backup arrives, they will. He's gotta go," Bishop said, still peering through the crack. "You pull the door. I'll take the shot."

"Got it." Kasey stepped around Bishop and gingerly took the handle. "Tell me when."

"On three. One, two, three," Bishop counted as she raised her Glock.

Kasey pulled the door wide, and Bishop fired twice. The shooter keeled over.

Bishop crouched low and entered the lobby. Kasey followed her in, scanning the lobby for signs of any other shooters.

The lobby was a mess. She counted three officers down, though they had put up a fight. Two of the masked attackers had been dropped just inside the front door.

"We're clear," Bishop called. "The rest of them must be upstairs still." She released the clip on her Glock and loaded a fresh magazine. Then she halted, staring at the man she had just shot. "Hey Kasey, we need more firepower. Take my Glock." She held out her weapon. "This needs to be the last time you're not carrying yours."

"Got it," Kasey answered, taking the weapon.

Bishop strode over to the downed shooter. Bending over, she grabbed the man's weapon. It was an MP5 sub-machine gun. Bishop checked the magazine. It was loaded.

"This will do nicely. Let's get Vida."

"Yep," Kasey said, her Glock looking like a toy next to Bishop's MP5. "Let's get him out of there."

MP5 in hand, Bishop charged across the lobby, past the elevators to the station's internal stairs. Kasey studied the floor readouts. They showed elevators on the second and third floor.

Opening the door to the stairs, Bishop checked the landing. "We're clear."

Bishop charged down the stairs, and Kasey followed after, guns raised and ready. Encountering no resistance, they arrived at the basement.

"The elevators were on the 2nd and 3rd floor. We should be clear. Let's grab Vida and get out of here," Kasey said.

"Yep, let's move. The quicker the better."

Kasey cracked open the door. The corridor leading to the morgue was empty.

She took it at a run. "Vida!"

She burst into the morgue. It was empty, the bodies of Wendel Samson and his accomplice had been moved to the refrigeration units.

"Vida, where are you?"

The room was empty, but the door leading to his office was shut. She darted to it, then twisted the handle and pushed it open.

She stopped short. "You have to be kidding me."

"What's up?" Bishop asked, catching up to Kasey.

"See for yourself," Kasey said, stepping aside.

Vida was sitting at his computer, headphones on, bobbing away as he pounded at his keyboard. Facing away from the door, he hadn't seen them enter.

Kasey made her way over to Vida and pulled on the earphones.

"Hey, hey," Vida yelled, swatting at Kasey's hand.

Vida turned in his chair and spotted Bishop. His eyes wandered from Bishop to the MP5 in her hands.

"What on earth is going on?"

"The station is under attack," Bishop replied. "We need to get out of here. Now!"

His eyes widened.

"W-what? Who?" he stammered.

"Skyler's friends," Kasey replied knowingly. "And they aren't playing games. We have officers down, maybe a dozen. The fighting is still going on upstairs, but when they are done there, they are going to come looking for Skyler. We can't be here when they do."

Vida whipped the headphones off and looked about frantically. Standing up, he grabbed his bag and began to stuff paperwork into it.

Bishop stepped in. "Vida, none of that matters now. Leave it. We'll be back."

"R-right," Vida said.

Kasey wrapped her arm around Vida's shoulders and steered him to the door. "Let's go."

Together, Kasey and Bishop guided him out of his office and through the morgue.

"Come on, Vida," Bishop said as they stepped into the hallway. "We have to pick up the pace. We're sitting ducks in here. We need to make it to the services entrance."

"Too late," Kasey said, pointing to the elevators.

They stopped dead. The elevator's floor readout was on the move.

Kasey's heart pounded in her chest. Her palms went clammy as she recalled the masked assailants that burst from the lift on the second floor.

She measured the distance to the elevator. The service entrance sat just beyond it.

There is no way we'll make it in time.

"Back into the morgue, Kasey," Bishop shouted. When Kasey didn't move, Bishop pushed her. "Now!"

"There's no way out," Kasey said. "We'll be stuck."

"We're better off in there than out here. It's a solid box of steel and concrete. We'll hold down the fort until backup arrives. Henley will have reached dispatch already. Reinforcements will be here in minutes. Ten at the most," Bishop reassured them.

"I remember the gala," Kasey whispered. "Ten minutes will be an eternity when the bullets start flying."

Bishop nodded. "Better get inside then."

Kasey watched as Bishop grabbed Vida and pushed him back into the morgue. Bishop paused at the door. Reaching over, she cut the lights in the hallway, plunging it into semi-darkness. Only the faint green glow of the exit sign provided any illumination.

Turning, Bishop pulled the door until it was almost closed.

Against the silence of the morgue, the crisp ding of the elevator rang clearly.

The Shinigami were here.

CHAPTER TWENTY-TWO

*B*ishop raised her MP5 to shoulder height and sighted her weapon on the elevator. As the elevator doors began to open, Bishop's trigger finger tightened. Bishop's mouth drew into a thin line.

"Welcome to the Ninth Precinct, you..."

The rest of Bishop's sentence was cut off by the sound of the MP5 opening up on the elevator. Even under pressure, Bishop was cool, calm, and collected, firing three round bursts into the elevator with clinical precision. Where others might have gone to town on elevator on full-auto, Bishop was making the most of every shot. Her calculated bursts turned the elevator into a death trap. The sound of the MP5 echoed around the morgue. The noise was deafening.

Kasey couldn't see the elevator with Bishop blocking the door, but every moment Bishop fired, her spirits soared.

Suddenly, gunfire erupted from the elevator.

Clearly, some of the Shinigami had survived Bishop's onslaught. Now they were pissed.

Bishop pushed the morgue's steel door shut. Bullets slammed into the other side of the door, setting off a cacophony of ricochets. The darkened corridor leading to the morgue was being shredded. Bishop slid the door's lock into place.

"That ought to give them something to think about," Bishop said as she turned to Kasey. Bullets continued to hammer into the door.

"How many are there?" Kasey asked.

"There was half a dozen. Now I'd say three, four tops. I dropped two of them for sure. If the third is still breathing, he won't be happy."

Another round of bullets slammed into the door.

"They can see the door's shut, so why do they keep firing?" Kasey asked.

"It's covering fire," Bishop replied not taking her eyes off the door. "If they want to advance on the morgue, they have little to no cover. They are trying to discourage me from opening the door and taking another shot at them."

"Will you?" Kasey prompted.

Bishop shook her head. "No, too great a risk. Hard to tell where they are situated until we crack the door, and when we do they will be ready for it. We're better off bedding down in here and waiting for reinforcements. They'll still have to breach the door and I didn't see any explosives, just guns. It may hold."

Bishop approached one of the examination tables. Without hesitation she threw her weight against the table, flipping it over. It slammed into the ground, the hollow clang reverberating through the morgue.

"What was that for?" Vida asked.

Bishop didn't slow down. Instead, she tipped over the second table. Surgical implements skittered across the floor as she replied, "Cover, Vida. We're going to need something to shield us just in case they make it through the door."

"Oh, they are coming through it," Kasey answered. "It's only a lock. That's not going to hold them for more than a few moments."

"What makes you so sure?" Bishop replied. "I just dropped two of them. Maybe three. That is going to slow them down."

"I don't think so. These are the guys that set Samson on the gala, and then gunned him down when they were through with him. They aren't going to care that we killed a few of their lackeys. They think we have Skyler, and when they work out she's dead, they are going to make sure we join her."

Bishop stopped and turned on Kasey. "What makes you so sure? We know next to nothing about this crew. They don't seem to give a damn about killing people, so what makes you think they care that much about one of their own? What makes her worth more than the three I just shot?"

Kasey shifted her weight slowly, leaning away from Bishop. She had answers to those questions, but there was no way Bishop would believe her, and Kasey wouldn't risk the ADI coming after Bishop.

It was bad enough that Vida had discovered her secret. She still hadn't worked out what she was going to do about him. If the Arcane Council discovered Vida, the consequences would be dire. They had warned as much after the incident with Brad Tescoe. If she kept up her current pattern, the whole Ninth Precinct would know her secret in no time.

If the Shinigami come through that door, I may not have a choice. The council's wrath beats certain death at this point.

With no answers she was willing to give, Kasey looked at Vida.

He simply stared back at her, his head tilted to one side. He seemed to be mouthing the words 'tell her' as his eyes bored into hers.

"Kasey," Bishop nudged. "What is it you aren't telling me?"

"Um," Kasey stalled, not sure what to say, she plunged her head into her hands.

"Kasey," Bishop pressed. "what's with the secrets? We're a team, remember?"

"It's got nothing to do with those gun toting maniacs, Bishop," Kasey said as she ran her hand through her hair to get it out of her face.

"Well, that's not entirely true," Vida interjected. "Come on, Kasey. It's Bishop. She needs to know, before they kill us all."

Bishop turned on him. "What do I need to know? You better tell me, Vida, or I swear…"

"You'll what?" he asked. "Kill me? Pretty sure the folks in the hall have that one covered."

Bishop fumed, pacing back and forward behind the upturned tables. "I can't believe it. I just can't believe it. I'm here risking my life and you two can't even tell me what is going on."

"Not every secret is meant to be shared, Bishop. Some things you are better off not knowing," Kasey said. Running for the other examination table.

Vida got the hint and scurried after her.

"If we get out of here, I'm not going to forget about this, Kasey. You're going to have to spill it eventually."

Kasey shook her head. "If we make it out of here alive, it's proof you didn't need to know in the first place."

Bishop's face was red, and her scowl deepened. It seemed as if she was about to break, but Kasey held out. She'd had no choice with Vida. She would not endanger Bishop if she could avoid it.

Surely backup will be here any moment.

Awkward silence descended on the morgue. Kasey strained to hear if there was any activity in the hallway. If the Shinigami were moving, they were doing so silently. All she could hear was the steady thumping of her own heart in her chest.

The handle on the door began to turn. Kasey gulped. Time was up.

A metallic click issued from the door as the handle stopped. The lock held.

Three heavy thuds rang out from the door.

"They're knocking?" Vida whispered. "Are you kidding me?"

"Shhh," Bishop replied, holding up a finger. "Don't answer. They are fishing for information."

There was a gurgling retch as someone in the hallway cleared their throat.

A man's voice filled the morgue. "We have come for Mina. Give her to us and we will leave. No one else needs to die today."

"That must be Skyler's real name," Bishop whispered. "Finally, a lead."

"Fat lot of good it will do us now," Kasey replied.

When no one responded, the voice called again. "This is your last chance. Give us Mina, or we will kill you and clamber over your corpse to get her back. The result will be the same."

Bishop racked her MP5 and readied it. Before Kasey could stop her, Bishop ignored her own advice and hurled her retort at the steel door. "Well, that's a shame. Your poor Mina got hit by a cab and now she's roadkill, or at least she was until these two clowns incinerated what was left of her."

"Your lies are pointless. We can sense her even now. Send her out, or we will come in and take her," the man said.

What do they mean sense? Kasey wondered.

"I would take the former. You won't live through the latter," a woman's voice added.

"Sense her?" Bishop asked. "Who the hell are these wierdos?"

"Shinigami," Vida answered. "Some bizarre Japanese death worshippers..."

"Vida!" Kasey clamped her hand over his mouth to cut him off.

"Enough, Kasey," Bishop snapped. "What's he talking about?"

The voice called again from the hall. "This is your last chance. Release Mina or die."

Bishop turned to Kasey. "Why are they so certain she's here? You guys sent the body to be destroyed, right?"

Vida looked at Kasey. "Well..."

"It was destroyed, but we didn't send it out," Vida replied. "We did it here just to be sure. What's left of her is in the medical incinerator."

Bishop's face was aghast. "Here? What? How?"

"It doesn't matter right now," Kasey replied. "She's gone. Nothing but ashes left, I assure you."

The woman's voice called again. "What is your choice? Your time is up. Mina or your lives."

"Bishop, even if we had her, they would still kill us. They have killed everyone they have come across. We just need to stall them for as long as we can."

"That, or trick them into doing something stupid," Bishop replied, taking aim at the door.

"What are you doing?" Kasey whispered.

Bishop paid her no heed. Instead, she hollered at the morgue's door, "We'd love to send Mina out. There's just one problem. She's dead."

"I think not," the husky voice replied. "As I told you before, we can sense her presence."

"I hate to disappoint you, but this is the morgue. All you can sense is her barbecued remains and there isn't much of them either. I could probably cram the ashes into a cup for you."

The voice bellowed through the door. "Enough! Surrender now. Your deaths, while certain, need not be painful."

Bishop was relentless. "Come on, guys, we're a police force not a funeral parlor. What will you do with them anyway? Bury them or scatter her at sea?"

The woman's voice lilted through the door. "Silence! I promise you will beg for mercy, and it will not come."

"Tempting," Bishop said, sighting her MP5 on the door. "Final offer, we're fresh out of urns, but if you give me a moment, I've got a half-finished Frappuccino here. I'll polish it off and we'll send out what's left of Mina."

The hall was silent.

"Hmm," Bishop muttered. "I was thinking that would have done the trick."

"What were you hoping for?" Vida whispered.

"I was hoping they would be angry enough to beat in the door. The less coordinated their assault, the better the chance we have of living through it."

"And now?" Vida asked.

"They are likely mustering their forces and preparing to blow the door," Bishop replied. "Keep your head down."

A tingle ran down Kasey's spine. Closing her eyes, she focused her mind on the sensation to be sure.

Magic, and it's building in power.

With one hand, she yanked Vida down until his butt hit the tile floor of the morgue.

"Ow," he protested.

"Bishop, get down. It's about to blow!" Kasey shouted.

"How do you know?" Bishop asked.

"Trust me!" Kasey pleaded.

"Says the one keeping secrets," Bishop replied, eyes fixed on the morgue's door.

"This is not the time, Bishop. If they blow that door, where do you think the shrapnel's going?"

Bishop sighed audibly as she sank to the floor

"Bakuhatsu Shiro!" bellowed the voice from hall.

A hellish screeching emanated from the door as it twisted and warped.

At the sound, Kasey shrank down behind her table.

The morgue's door buckled under the arcane onslaught and shattered inward, showering the morgue in steel and shrapnel.

CHAPTER TWENTY-THREE

The shower of steel turned the morgue into a killing field. Shrapnel ricocheted throughout the confined space. One large slab of steel slammed into the table Kasey was hiding behind.

As the room went still, Bishop leaned around the end of the table and emptied her MP5 into the doorway.

Kasey peeked over the table in time to see two black clad acolytes collapse. A third burst into the morgue, firing her weapon at Bishop.

Bishop dropped behind the table as the storm of steel struck it.

With Bishop under fire, Kasey drew a bead on the woman and fired three shots in quick succession.

The first missed but the second and third found their mark. The woman dropped to the floor but continued firing haphazardly until her clip ran dry.

Another form appeared in the doorway. Kasey recognized him from the second floor. The Shinigami wore his hair drawn back in a traditional top knot. His eyes were fixed on Kasey and the gun in her hand.

Kasey turned her weapon on the Shinigami.

"*Mamore*," the Shinigami commanded.

The language was unintelligible to Kasey, but she'd seen enough to know a world of hurt was coming her way.

She pulled the trigger.

There was a wet thud as the bullet stopped just shy of the Shinigami, hovering harmlessly in the air before him.

Kasey squeezed the trigger again. The bullet came to a halt only an inch from the first. She continued firing, quickly unloading the weapon at the Shinigami in front of her. Soon a dozen rounds hovered before him.

She pulled the trigger again. A metallic click echoed from the Glock.

Empty.

The corners of the Shinigami's mouth edged upward into a smile as he raised his hand. *"Ose!"*

The spell struck Kasey and the table she was hiding behind. The table screeched across the floor, while Kasey was thrown across the room. Bishop's Glock flew out of her hand and skittered across the ground.

Kasey groaned as she slammed into the morgue's wall and fell to the floor.

"What was that?" Bishop muttered, looking aghast.

The blonde Shinigami appeared in the doorway.

"Not so feisty now, are you?" The woman seethed as she bore down on Bishop. "You normals and your guns. You rely on such worthless tools to do your will. Now look at you. Your ignorance is almost amusing."

With her gun empty, Bishop hurled the weapon at the woman.

The Shinigami ducked. The MP5 clattered along the floor.

She swept both hands through the air and cried out, *"Hinotama."*

A wisp of fire materialized above her hand. The wisp flickered and grew into a sphere of flames broiling in the air before her. With a flick of her wrist, the woman hurled the fireball at Bishop.

With a gasp, Bishop dove down behind the table as the flames washed over it.

"What was it you did to Mina? Something about a barbecue. I assure you, you will share her fate."

Kasey struggled to breath. She'd been winded when she struck the wall. Fighting the burning sensation in her chest she scanned the room.

A circle of fire erupted around Bishop, cutting her off from Kasey or Vida.

The male Shinigami turned his attention to Bishop as well. "I imagine you are beginning to realize the price you will pay. Your life for Mina's. Consider yourself fortunate. In times past, entire cities have burned for the transgression you committed today. Know that each of the officers who died here today, did so because of you. This is the price you pay for defying the Gods of Death."

Bishop's face was white. Beads of sweat ran down her face. With each passing moment, the circle of flames constricted.

"Look on the bright side," the woman chided. "At least you won't live to see your city burn."

"Focus, Eriko. This is not the time nor place to bandy about the master's ministrations."

"What does it matter, Hideyo? It's not like they will live to speak of it."

The flames grew higher. Bishop searched for an escape, but there was none.

"What, no more witty retorts?" Eriko taunted. "I'll settle for your last words."

Bishop ignored her. Instead focusing on the shifting flames licking closer and closer every second.

Kasey locked eyes with Bishop, as the flames grew brighter she could wait no longer. Kasey ignored her exhaustion and rose to her feet.

Eriko continued. "Oh, what's wrong? Cat got your tongue? Funny how that always happens in the end. Courage always fades in the face of certain death."

A river of sweat ran down Bishop's face as the flames licked at her trousers.

"Goodbye, officer, you were fun while you lasted," Eriko teased.

There were some prices Kasey wasn't willing to pay to protect her secret. Losing Bishop was one of them. Kasey cleared her mind except for a single thought. The murderous Eriko before her.

"*Trydanu!*" Kasey's bellow shook the morgue. She was on her feet now. Her right hand quivered as it formed a conduit for the arcane energy surging madly through her being.

Both Shinigami turned. Hideyo's face was impassive. Eriko, on the other hand, was caught flatfooted. It seemed they had supposed Kasey was down for the count. The shock of her reappearance was outshone by the incantation she had just uttered. A surge of power akin to a lightning bolt leapt from Kasey's outstretched hand.

Hideyo was fast.

"*Mamore,*" he chanted, raising his protective barrier once more.

Eriko was caught between her execution of Bishop and Kasey's unexpected arcane assault.

The bolt caught her in the chest and blasted her off her feet. She tumbled across the floor of the morgue before coming to a halt. Her body convulsed involuntarily as the energy raced to ground itself.

"What a bitch," Kasey exclaimed as she bore down on Hideyo. "Using magic to torment normals. It's pathetic. To think you use your powers to beguile, confuse, and enslave those who don't know any better. Let's see how you fare against your own kind."

"Our kind?" Hideyo spat. "Don't be deluded. Were you to live three lifetimes, you would still be a child to me. You know nothing of us. If you did, you wouldn't have dared to defy us."

"Don't I?" Kasey answered. "You use your magic to masquerade as gods while you sow death and discord among the ignorant. You made a big mistake coming here, Hideyo. New York will be the end of you."

"Child, please. I have been a Shinigami since before you were a glint in your father's eye. You may have taken Eriko by surprise, but you won't get lucky twice."

Kasey laughed. "I already have. First Mina, now Eriko. Do you still think it's luck?" I have news for you, Hideyo, and it's all bad. I'm prescient. Why do you think your Master didn't come himself? He's already sent one assassin after me and failed. Now you idiots come bumbling into our station, without even knowing I'm here. It's almost embarrassing."

"Lies," Hideyo chafed.

"Are they? Take your best shot and we'll see. I've seen every way that this might play out, Hideyo," Kasey bluffed, "and there isn't one where you walk out that door alive."

Hideyo went quiet. His eyes were fixed on her, but his confidence seemed to be waning.

Bishop seized the opportunity and dove for her pistol. She had a spare magazine in her hand.

Hideyo's eyes followed Bishop as she slid across the tiles

"*Shi-ne!*" he shouted.

Kasey recognized the incantation. It was the same words Mina had been chanting when she had been struck by the taxi earlier.

A bolt of green energy hurtled at Bishop.

"*Tarian,*" Kasey chanted.

A shimmering silver shield appeared, hovering over Bishop's prostrate form. The green bolt glanced off the shield and struck the floor mere feet from where Bishop lay. Tiles shattered in a spray of ceramic shrapnel. A plume of green smoke rose from the scarred floor.

The luminescent green smoke was only too familiar to Kasey.

My vision. The attack on New York. That is the same smoke I saw. It is a magical attack. I knew it!

Hideyo seized on Kasey's distraction. "*Ose!*"

Kasey's heart raced. She dove to the side to avoid the blast, but the energy still clipped her shoulder and knocked her onto her back. Pain surged through her spine.

Hideyo strode toward her.

"*Shi-ne!*" he shouted, striding toward her.

The luminescent blast split the air as it arced between them. This time, the emerald energy was a prolonged lance of power boring toward Kasey.

"*Tarian,*" Kasey chanted feverishly, focusing on the space between her and the advancing Shinigami.

Her shield materialized in the nick of time, absorbing the blast as it struck the protective barrier dead center. The force of the impact shook Kasey to her core. It required all her concentration to maintain the spell. Sweat ran down her brow as she struggled against Hideyo.

When the barrage ended, she breathed a sigh of relief.

Her shield dissipated, revealing Hideyo standing over her. In his hand, a knife gleamed brightly under the morgue's ceiling lights. Clearly, he had tired of the duel.

He drove the knife toward her. She tried to roll out of the way, but her muscles seized. She could not force herself to move.

Suddenly, Hideyo's smile twisted into a grimace. Then, he howled in agony as he turned, revealing a surgical scalpel buried in his back. Vida stood wincing as he backed away from the Shinigami.

Hideyo turned his attention on Vida but came to a halt.

Kasey had caught him by the ankle.

With her mind racing, Kasey uttered the first incantation she could think of. *"Berwi!"*

Boil. Kasey often used it to reheat her coffee. Hideyo was considerably larger than the average latte, but the incantation's effect was immediate. His skin began to welter and pucker as his blood boiled within him. Hideyo's flesh turned an angry red as Kasey's spell cooked him from the inside out.

He howled in pain as he lunged at Vida.

A gunshot echoed through the morgue. Hideyo jerked as a bullet struck him in the back. Another gunshot followed. The Shinigami collapsed at Vida's feet. Kasey turned to see Bishop lying on the floor, Glock raised, a faint wisp of smoke rising from its barrel.

"Nice shot," Kasey said as she laid her head back against the cool tiles.

Bishop struggled to her feet. "W-what the hell was that, Kasey? Who are these people? And what was with the fire and the lightning?"

There was no way out. Bishop had seen enough magic to last a lifetime. Wiping her memories simply wasn't an option for Kasey; that level of magical manipulation lay far beyond her abilities. She might scramble Bishop's mind by accident. It wasn't worth the risk.

Even if I could, would I want to?

There was a loneliness to living with one foot in the World of Magic and one foot in the real world. Part of Kasey was relieved that Vida had discovered her secret. The other was terrified of what it meant, or what would happen if the ADI discovered her failure.

I'll have to cross that bridge when I come to it.

"Kasey?" Bishop prodded.

"Promise to hear me out, before you declare me insane?" Kasey asked.

Bishop set down her pistol. "Only if you promise that it will be the truth. I'm tired of the lies."

Kasey considered Bishop's words. "I can do that."

Bishop looked about the morgue. "Then, in light of what I've just seen, I'm willing to keep an open mind."

Kasey didn't get up. She simply began her tale. "Bishop, there is more to the world than what you know. Hiding in plain sight is the greatest secret humanity has to offer. Magic. Wielded by those who can speak the ancient tongues, its secrets have been passed from generation to generation. In the dark ages we were almost purged from existence. Any of our people that survived withdrew from the public eye and safeguarded its existence.

"We hid from the world and magic thrived. Now we share the world. We do so without the violence and persecution we once faced but only because of the secrets that we keep. I know that the discovery of our kind will bring back the destruction and death we have faced before."

Bishop shook her head. "What are you saying?"

"I'm saying, that I'm a witch—a real one—and you can't tell another soul."

CHAPTER TWENTY-FOUR

*B*ishop stared down at Kasey. With the Shinigami dead, the morgue was silent.

Kasey's explanation hung heavily in the air.

"Bishop?" Kasey said, her lip quivered as she waited for a reply.

Bishop paced back and forth, staring at the morgue's floor.

"Bishop, talk to me," Kasey said.

"Damn it, Kasey, give me a minute. For my entire life, I thought I knew the world and my place in it, and now these psychos appear wielding flames and lightning, and you tell me it's magic. I saw it with my own eyes and yet... Kasey...this changes everything."

Kasey lifted herself off the ground. "You're telling me. I live with this every day. For years, it was a burden, but now I've been using my gifts to save lives."

"Gifts?" Bishop asked. "There is more than one? More than the magic I just saw?"

"Yes. It's a little harder to believe. Even among my kind."

"What can be harder to believe than this?" Bishop asked pointing at the devastation the magic had caused in the morgue.

"I see visions," Kasey answered. "I have since I was a child."

"Visions. What kind of visions?" Bishop asked.

"When I come in contact with people, there is a chance I'll see a vision. Scenes from their future or their past. I cannot control when or where, but I see them nonetheless. I've been using them to help us solve cases and catch murderers. That is how I learned of Collin's true identity. I saw a vision of him visiting Lincoln Strode before he died."

"You can see the future?" Bishop asked.

"Don't get your hopes up. I can't control the visions."

"So, no chance of this week's lotto numbers?" Bishop chuckled.

"I'm afraid not. If I could do that, I wouldn't be busting my ass as a Medical Examiner."

"I suppose not. Is that what you meant when you told them you had seen how today would end? Did you know this was coming? Did you know they would attack the station?"

"No, Bishop, I only discovered Skyler's true identity minutes before the attack. My mother warned me of the Shinigami and what they would do, if they tracked Skyler here. We tried to destroy the body, but we were too late. They were already on their way."

"Then your mention of a vision earlier when you threatened him?"

"I was bluffing," Kasey answered.

Bishop shook her head. "One day, you are going to overplay your hand, Kasey."

Kasey smiled. "Not today, Bishop. Those demented lunatics got what was coming to them."

"What were they?" Bishop asked. "You called them Shinigami? What is a Shinigami?"

"The Shinigami are a coven of Japanese witches and wizards. They are obsessed with death, and they use their powers against normal people. They kill people to learn about death and its effects on the human soul. They are murderers, every one of them.

"If the stories are to be believed, their dark organization has been responsible for the death of countless people. Entire cities have been destroyed by them. The Japanese believe them to be emissaries or spirits sent by the God of Death, sent to draw mortals into his presence. We are fortunate that they had no idea Skyler was dead, otherwise they may have simply destroyed the station and everyone in it."

"What are they doing here in New York?" Bishop asked.

"I believe they are planning an attack on the city. I saw a vision of it as a child. The city devastated by magic. At first, I thought it was a nightmare, but I have seen it over and over since then. Now I am convinced it is a tragedy that still lies in the future. Danilo, the man we knew as agent Collins, was hired by the Shinigami to kill me. My vision of an attack was well known in the Academy. Stories of that attack must've reached the Shinigami and they sent Danilo to silence me. If the Shinigami are here, the attack must be drawing nearer."

"Collins was a part of this too?"

"Unfortunately. He was killing anyone in the city who matched my description. I changed my name when I fled the Academy, so they had no idea who I was. He was simply eliminating anyone who could be me."

"He was just guessing?" Bishop asked, her eyes wide.

"I'm afraid so. The Shinigami are determined to carry out their attack. All of these events are connected—Danilo, the shooting at the Gala, Cyrus' assassination. All of them are linked. Cyrus was the head of law enforcement for the Arcane Council."

Bishop and Vida exchanged glances.

"The Arcane Council are the body that govern magic users," Kasey explained. "We can't just have witches and wizards running around unsupervised. Who knows what chaos would ensue. The Arcane Council regulate affairs here in the United States, and Cyrus was an important part of that council."

Bishop nodded. "You think they killed him to pave way for the attack?"

"I'm almost certain of it," Kasey replied. "They were willing to kill dozens of innocent people just to make Cyrus look like an accident. They don't want people to know what they are up to as they plot their attack. It's coming Bishop, I've seen it. We need to stop them before others get hurt."

"How many are there?" Bishop answered.

"I'm not exactly sure," Kasey responded, biting on her lower lip.

"I think I can answer that," Vida said. The head medical examiner was still trembling from the fight with the Shinigami. He was leaning on the upturned examination table for support.

Both Kasey and Bishop turned on Vida. "How?"

"Well, I can't be sure," Vida said with a shrug, "but I was doing research while you were upstairs with Bishop. The World of Magic may be a secret, but the Shinigami are not. There are hundreds of websites devoted to them. They are one of the most well-known branches of Japanese lore and mythology. There are stories, comics, anime, and even a movie devoted to them.

"Normal people may not know the truth of these Shinigami, but one thing is consistent. That is the number. In Japanese, the word shi has two meanings. First it means death, as we are aware, but secondly it also means the number four. As a result, the number four is considered to be an unlucky or a bad omen. Many apartment buildings do not label the fourth floor, but they simply skip it and number the floors one, two, three, five and so on. If there was going to be a number significant to the Shinigami, surely it would be the number four."

"I think you're onto something. In my vision, I heard four voices. We know that the one known as Skyler to us, or Mina to them, is dead. Hideyo and Eriko are too. We just saw to that. That makes three." Kasey nodded as she raised three fingers.

"Leaving us with one," Bishop stated.

"Indeed," Kasey answered as she looked at Bishop, "the one they know as Master. He is behind it all. If we can stop him, we will stop the attack. Everything depends on it."

"You didn't happen to get a look of him in your vision?" Bishop shook her head as she spoke. "I hear myself saying the words, but it still sounds weird. Visions, magic, it's a lot to swallow."

"Unfortunately not. Skyler was bowing, and she never looked up from the ground. It wouldn't have helped us, anyway," Kasey replied

"Why not? Bishop answered.

"The Shinigami are adept at using their magic to disguise their identity. It is the reason we've had so much trouble closing this case. The man I thought was the waiter at the gala, the man that shot Cyrus, he was really a Shinigami who was imitating Ben's face with magic. The man that we thought was Stevens in the warehouse, another Shinigami.

"When we were chasing Skyler, she even briefly stole your appearance, Bishop. That was why I froze in the hallway of her building. I was looking at her but all I could see was you pointing a gun at me. It's a good thing you showed up when you did."

Bishop resumed pacing. "So, this master could be anyone?"

"Yes," Kasey answered. "We're going to have to tread carefully. He could be anyone and he's plotting to blow up our city."

"Can't you go to this Arcane Council?" Bishop suggested.

"Not yet. I don't know who we can trust. We must keep this between us until we know more, and remember, you can't tell a soul about me. Not my visions or my magic. The Council will stop at nothing to protect our secret and I don't want anything to happen to either of you."

"So where do we start?" Bishop asked.

"We need to clear out the station, make sure none of their acolytes are still roaming around upstairs," Kasey said pointing to the floors above.

"Definitely. We'll also need to get medical attention for any of our officers who survived the attack. Most importantly, we need to scour this morgue of any trace of the Shinigami. As their magic fades, their appearance changes. We saw it with Skyler's body, that's why we had to destroy it. We can't have anyone else learning what they truly are. Can you imagine the panic that would cause?"

"Yeah. The city would go into a panic. Knowing that somewhere out there, a wizard is planning to destroy the city. I get your point, let's do it. Reinforcements are gonna be here any moment. How do you plan to clean this up?" Bishop asked.

Kasey put an arm around both Bishop and Vida and steered them to the door.

"The same way I cleaned the scene at my apartment," Kasey replied

"Wait…" Vida began, "didn't your apartment burn down?"

"Yep, but that might have been less accidental than I initially lead on."

"My morgue!" Vida exclaimed as he tried to dig in his heels.

Kasey and Bishop shoved him through the door.

Bishop turned to Kasey. "What, exactly, were you trying to hide at your apartment? Collins was a killer but we all knew that, so why burn the place down?"

"I didn't want anyone looking too closely at the body."

Bishop raised an eyebrow. "Why is that?"

"Because..." Kasey paused, unsure just how much she should reveal. Tired of the lies, she took a deep breath and said, "He was a werewolf."

"A Werewolf!" Vida shouted.

"Now you're just messing with me," Bishop replied.

"I wish I was," Kasey replied. "Collins was a Werewolf and I killed him with a magic spear. I figured that would be pretty hard to explain away,"

Bishop and Vida exchanged a disbelieving glance as they started down the hall.

"Gee, this truth thing is pretty liberating!" Kasey exclaimed. "I feel like a giant load has been lifted from my shoulders."

Bishop shook her head.

"Just give me a moment to take care of this," Kasey said, stopping in the hallway and turning back to face the morgue. She raised her hands, channeling her power. "*Pêl Tân!*"

Flames leapt from her outstretched palms and poured through the doorway into the morgue. Determined to erase every sign of the Shinigami, she gave it everything she had.

The blaze grew into a swirling inferno.

Soon the morgue was consumed by the blaze, along with everything in it. Satisfied that the fire would do its job, Kasey ceased her channeling.

Turning from the blaze, she put her arms around Vida and Bishop and directed them toward the stairs.

Stepping over the body of one of the acolytes, Kasey let out a sigh of relief. "What a day."

"Do you have any idea how much paperwork you just caused us, Kasey? We're going to need a new morgue," Vida stammered.

Kasey nodded. "Ah, but think of all the other paperwork I just saved us, Vida. Now those guys won't be needing an autopsy."

"You're crazy!" Vida replied.

Kasey smiled. "Perhaps. Good thing we're on the same side. That last Shinigami is in for a world of hurt."

"Hopefully he is as arrogant as that lot. If he is, he'll never see it coming," Bishop replied.

"Perhaps not," Kasey said, "but I will."

The End

When a vision reveals the brutal murder one of New York's elite, Kasey finds herself fighting to save his life. Fate can be a fickle mistress though, where one life is spared, another is required. Who will pay the price? Find out in When Death Knocks, available now.

https://www.samuelcstokes.com/conjuringcoroner

Want to be a VIP?

VIP's get early access to all the good stuff, including exclusive giveaways, signed editions, exclusive pre-release parties, and free books! Click the link below to join today.

Become A VIP - https://readerlinks.com/l/959935

YOU ARE THE DIFFERENCE

I hope you enjoyed *Life is for the Living*. I'm sure you can see that Kasey's saga is beginning to unfold. What will become of her as the deadly plot against New York comes to fruition? I guess we'll find out together. In the meantime, I wanted to ask you something.

As a self-published author, I don't have the huge marketing machine of a traditional publisher behind me. In fact, it's just me, my laptop and a hunger to share my stories with the world.

Since I began this journey though, I have discovered I have something far greater on my side. **You. The incredible readers that share my worlds and my love for a good book.**

Every time you send a message or email, tell a friend about my series or share it on social media it helps me reach readers and continue to bring you more stories!

Also, your honest reviews of my books help other readers take a chance on me. It is the #1 thing you can do to help me (and Kasey) out.

If you have enjoyed this book, I would love it if you could spend a minute or two to leave a review for me (it can be as short or as long as you like), the link below will take you to the right page.

https://www.samuelcstokes.com/conjuringcoroner

Thank you, your support makes all the difference!

Until next time!

S. C. Stokes

P.S. I know many readers are hesitant to reach out to an author, fearing that they might get ignored. I am a reader at heart and know how you feel. I respond personally to every Facebook message and every email I receive.

You can find me on:
    Facebook
    Bookbub
    Email: samuel@samuelcstokes.com

You can also visit my website where you can join the VIP's and get some free books and other amazing goodies.

Scroll on for an exclusive preview of Conjuring A Coroner 3: When Death Knocks.

WHEN
DEATH
KNOCKS

S. C. STOKES

AN EXCLUSIVE PREVIEW OF WHEN DEATH KNOCKS

At that moment, one maniacal wizard plotted the destruction and misery of millions of souls. New York City, and everyone in it was in imminent danger. With countless lives hanging in the balance, Kasey couldn't help but think of those that had already been lost.

The assembly around Kasey fell silent as a single figure rose to his feet. His brief walk from his chair to the podium was made in measured strides. The man was dressed in his navy-blue NYPD dress uniform, from the toe of his brightly polished shoes to the embroidered tip of his police cover. The three gold stars embroidered into his lapel, designated him as the chief of one of New York City's many police precincts.

To Kasey, he was more than just a police chief. He was her chief. He had taken a chance on her, even though her world had been falling apart. There were few people in New York City willing to stand up to the political machine of the Ainsleys and their money. West had not yielded an inch. He had sheltered her from the storm.

Kasey was close enough that she could see his puffy eyes and his red tinged nose. Her heart broke knowing what the chief had endured these past few days. She watched as his lip quivered ever so slightly.

Reaching the podium, the chief straightened, and drew in a deep breath. The gray sprinkled through his mustache and hair only served to highlight his distinguished appearance. Chief West was a highly decorated officer and a pillar of the community. Few were the foes brave or foolish enough to cross his path. The chief stood, silently waiting at the podium. The improvised stage had been hastily erected in the center of Madison Square Garden.

The Garden had hosted countless events over its illustrious lifetime. From charity galas, to sporting matches to rock concerts. John Lennon, Patrick Ewing, and Elton John, Madison Square Garden had seen them all. Several times it had even hosted the NBA finals and the Stanley cup finals simultaneously. Cheering fans were known to drown the immense arena in a cacophony of revelry as they cheered their home-town heroes to glory.

Every seat was filled today, but no one was cheering. The entire arena was melancholy. Kasey waited in sobering silence for the Chief to begin.

His gaze scanned across the caskets lining the space before the stage. Eighteen caskets, each adorned with a flag of the United States of America, the country its officers had served so valiantly.

The normally steely-eyed chief reached up and swept a tear from his eye.

Taking a deep breath, he began, "As you are aware, I am Jonathan West, Chief of the NYPD's Ninth District. The Fighting Ninth,"

His anguish was clearly visible, from the wrinkled corners of his eyes to his tightly drawn upper lip.

"You have all heard and seen the senseless violence that befell our precinct last week. These caskets that you see before you today hold the bodies of our valiant men and women, who gave their lives in defense of this city, in defense of you. These eighteen brave men and women made the greatest sacrifice one can make. They did so for you, and for me. They did so, so that this city would be a safer place for each of us. For our families. Each and every one of them were an officer worthy of the uniform which they wore proudly. We mourn them as a precinct, as a city, and as a nation. We mourn them as our family."

Kasey felt tears well up in her eyes as she thought of her fallen colleagues.

The chief continued. "It is my intention that a monument will be erected in the lobby of the Ninth Precinct, where their badges will remain as a memorial of their courage, heroism, and sacrifice. Let all who come to that place, now and forevermore, know that they laid down their lives for their country.

"As for the cowardly organization who perpetrated this act of senseless violence, I am here to raise the warning voice."

Kasey's heart skipped a beat.

Chief West grasped the podium with both hands. "You are here in our city, in our home. The NYPD will not be bullied nor beaten into submission. We will fight you with every fiber of our being and with every breath in our body. We will hunt you down and you will answer for your crimes. With you all as my witness, I swear that today, just as in days past, that we will stand in defense of our people and our city. New York will never give in. It will never surrender, and neither will we. Flee while you still can. Today we bury our fallen and tomorrow we're coming for you. You may have begun this bloodshed, but we will end it and you."

He straightened to his full height and drew a deep breath. "Would you all please stand, as the Honor guards carry our officers to the vehicles that will bear them to their final resting place. Internment services will be directed by the families of these brave men and women. We ask that you respect their wishes and that you wait for them to depart the building before you attempt to return home.

"My brave officers of the Fighting Ninth, rest in peace, you might be gone but you'll never be forgotten."

Stepping to the side of the pulpit, Chief West snapped a salute. The assembly rose to its feet. The Honor guard consisting of the surviving officers of the Fighting Ninth took their places beside the caskets. As one they raised the caskets and bore them from the arena.

As the funeral procession filed from the arena, the deep resonating notes of bagpipes filled the stadium. The families of the fallen officers wept openly as each soulful chord of Amazing Grace echoed through the vast stadium.

Kasey's heart went out to the Chief, and to her fallen comrades. The attack on the precinct had been swift and brutal. Together with Bishop and Vida she had only narrowly escaped death herself. What

Chief West and the other officers of the Ninth Precinct didn't know, was the true reason behind the attack.

The Shinigami and their thuggish acolytes had attacked the precinct in a misguided attempt to rescue one of their own, Mina, who had died while Kasey and Bishop had been trying to arrest her. Mina had been run down by a taxi and taken to the Ninth Precinct for her autopsy.

Two more had died during the attack on the precinct, along with more than a dozen acolytes they had brought with them.

The Shinigami were a cabal of Japanese wizards bent on destruction. The Shinigami traversed the world inflicting misery and devastation in order to study the forbidden art of necromancy. Obsessed with death and the ability to live forever, the Shinigami pursued their goal with single-minded intent. At home in Japan, the Shinigami were feared as the harbingers of death. Now the Shinigami had come to New York. What had brought them to the city, was not entirely clear, but Kasey's gut told her there was a connection with the coming attack on the city. Ever since she was a child, she had been afflicted with visions of the attack. The city being devastated by explosions as arcane forces tore the city apart. Recent events had led her to believe the attack was imminent. The Shinigami's arrival certainly heralded ill tidings for the city.

Fortunately for New York, Kasey knew it was coming and she was doing everything in her power to stop it.

Of the four Shinigami, three of them were now dead. Only one remained: The Master.

The same Master who had hired Danilo Lelac to kill her. He was also behind the plot to destroy the city. Unfortunately, the Shinigami possessed the means to alter their appearance with magic. As far as Kasey knew, the Master could be anyone.

Searching for one maniacal wizard in a city of millions was a monumental task, but failure would mean death. For Kasey, and for every living soul in the city.

Join Kasey in *When Death Knocks* today.

https://www.samuelcstokes.com/conjuringcoroner

Made in the USA
Middletown, DE
01 December 2022

16680684R00123